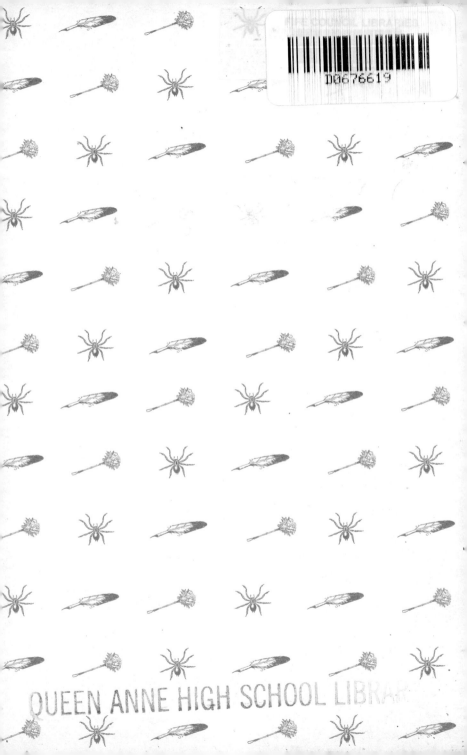

JIRION'S
SECRET JOURNAL

Jenny Sullivan

PONT

First Impression – 2005

ISBN 1 84323 460 2

© Text: Jenny Sullivan
© Illustrations: Brett Breckon

This book is published with the financial support of the
Welsh Books Council.

*Printed in Wales at
Gomer Press, Llandysul, Ceredigion SA44 4QL*

Foreword

This novel is set in Llancaiach Fawr Manor, Nelson, South Wales.

If you visit Llancaiach Fawr Manor with your family or your school, you will almost certainly meet some of the people mentioned in this book: perhaps Bleddyn ap Thomas, the Cook; John Bolitho, Colonel Prichard's Valet; Steffan Mathias, his Agent; Elisabeth Proude, Seamstress; Catrin Howell; Hannah Saer; Enid Samuel; Mrs Ann Thomas, the Housekeeper; Sian Thomas, the Goose-girl or Sarah Parry, the Lady's Maid. You are unlikely to meet Tirion or Ifor, the Spit-boy, although Ifor may be mentioned by some of his friends in the House.

Throughout the book you will find little numbers in the middle of the story, which refer to footnotes at the bottom of the page. These may not directly have to do with the story, but they are Interesting Bits and Pieces about what it was like living in the seventeenth century, and Tirion and I wanted you to know them.

My grateful thanks to all the people at Llancaiach who gave me access, information and their precious time.

JS

This book is dedicated to all Living History re-enactors, especially those at Llancaiach, whose enthusiasm helps to bring our history to life for us; to my daughter Kirsty, Education Officer at the Museum of London, and my daughter Stephanie, who re-enacts the past at different venues in Ireland. And for this year's new sons-in-law, Conall and Darren.

Chapter One

I was tired, cold, and my bum hurt.[1]

'Nearly there, look,' Wil-bach said, flapping the reins on old Mari's broad backside. 'Just round this bend and there we shall be.'

This morning in the icy grey dawn, I'd been excited by the prospect of a new life, terrified to be leaving home and going so far away, afraid-and-excited at being a working grown-up person,[2] and sad at leaving my Mam. But I am not sad at all to be leaving Master Ieuan ap Evan, my rotten stepfather and his horrid son. I'll tell you more about them later, but it will have to be in my Secret Journal. I promised Mam that I'd write a journal and take it home to her when I go back on my days off, but I don't want her to read what I really think of Master Eyes and Ears, as I call him. He is a horrible bully, and he must have the last word in all things. She

---

1 Bum was a perfectly good word in 1645.

2 Tirion is 10, which is quite old to be going off to work for those days. Steffan Mathias, whom you will meet later, began working at Llancaiach Fawr as a messenger when he was only 5.

married him because we were poor and without a home after Dada died of plague, but I wish there had been some other way for us to live.[3]

I shall write this, my Secret Journal, as if I am writing to an imaginary friend. In it I shall put secrets, and things that I would never dare to say aloud. But when I get old, perhaps my memory will fail as dear Wil-bach's does, and I want to remember all I can about my first time away from home.

There may even be things that I hear while I am attending my Mistress, Colonel Prichard's wife. These I should not tell anyone. But I *can* write them to my imaginary friend, because then no one will see but myself!

I could not have kept a journal at home, for my stepfather has eyes and ears not only in the back of his head but all round too, because he always knew when I was even *thinking* of doing something he didn't approve of. And since he didn't approve of much at all, and especially didn't approve of me, I got beaten, although his own son, Siôn, could do just as he liked and get away with it.

---

[3] She had no choice but to marry. A woman had no rights in law – if she had any money her father controlled it until she married, then her husband. If he went and died, it was back to Dad again, or even her brothers!

I expect that you are surprised to learn that I can read and write.[4] Most girls can't, but my Mam was a parson's daughter, and her Dada taught her to read, and my Dada was a parson, and so both my parents taught me, and I am glad that they did. Reading is a comfort and a joy, no matter how sad a person may be. Reading takes me into other, wonderful worlds. It would be marvellous to have ten, twenty, a hundred books to read instead of the few that my parents owned. If the book is a sad book, mind, then it will make you cry – but it is good crying, because it is not real, only a book, and as soon as the covers are closed, well then, you can be happy again.

My Dada, before he died, thought it was a Good Thing for girls to read, even though our brains are so much smaller than men's. He believed that whatever space there is inside, any one of God's people should be filled with Godly knowledge and anything else that we care to learn about.

'Tirion,' he would say, his eyes twinkly the way they were before he was ill and died, 'Tirion, if your

---

[4] Most girls of good family didn't learn to read, write or add up. Instead, they learned to paint, to play musical instruments, to dance and to sew. There was a craze in the 17th century for stitching beads onto bags . . . Imagine that as your whole life's entertainment!

husband should object to his wife being educated, then your husband will be an ass and a fool. An educated woman is a worthy companion to any man,' and my Mam agreed.

Master Eyes and Ears on the other hand did not. He thinks that women have brains enough only to have a dozen children and keep house. According to him, too much learning will only confuse us, and eventually our brains will explode like one of Oliver Cromwell's cannon. However, I think *my* brain is a lot bigger than the one inside his son's skull. Siôn's brain is probably the size of a very small pea and likely rattles when he walks. If that is not an Unkind Thought, in which case I hope God will forgive me. Unless God is still trying to forgive me for biting Master Eyes and Ears Very Hard last time he beat me.

Master Eyes caught me reading a pamphlet[5] that I had picked up – it was lying in the street. It was very rude about Cromwell, and it earned me a thrashing with the whippy bundle of sticks Master Eyes keeps

---

[5] Such pamphlets made important people Very Cross, because they usually said lots of shockingly bad things about them (some of which may have been true), and were published and sold very cheaply to anyone who wanted one, rather like today's newspapers.

in the corner for the purpose. Which is partly why my bum is sore right now. It's also partly because the seat of Wil-bach's best wagon is wooden and hard and full of splinters, and it's been a long, cold journey today, the Sunday before the First Monday after Twelfth Day, *Dydd Gŵyl Geilwad, at y bara haidd a'r bacsau.*[6] That is the day we stop celebrating Christmas and go back to work. Or in my case, start work. And not before time, Master E and E would say, since in two years' time I shall be twelve, and old enough to consent to marriage.

Or not. Mind you, if Old Eyes has anything to do with it, then he will probably beat me to make me marry someone horrible, like himself. So better I should be away and out of it, where he can't see me, and he might forget about finding me a husband.

Wil-bach does not talk much: but he's warm to huddle up against, even if he does smell of horse-sweat – and his own, too. But then, most people do. I just hope he hasn't got too many fleas, because I had a wash all over last night, even though it is only January and not proper washing season. I nearly froze solid while I was doing it. There were lots of drowned fleas in the water, after: little black speckles

---

6 Plough Monday, when it was usual to start eating ordinary food again and go back to work after Christmas.

11

in the grey scum of Mam's home-made soap. I think I got rid of most of them, because I have hardly scratched at all today. Unless, like me, they are so cold that they are too stiff to bite!

It's strange: when Master Eyes told me that I was to come to Llancaiach Fawr to work, he said it was because he was fed up with feeding and clothing a useless girl, and that it was high time I went out into the world to earn my living and help support the family. Perhaps he thought I would scream and cry and beg not to be sent away from my Mam. But I didn't. Mind you, half of me wants to be back in my Mam's arms and safe, although Master Eyes didn't approve of that, either, being a sign of weakness when I should Trust in the Lord and put All Else Aside, being a great girl of ten years. The other half is excited and wants to run to meet this new life.

Master Eyes recommended me to his friend Bleddyn ap Thomas, who is Cook at Llancaiach Fawr, and he has spoken to the Steward, and there now, I am a grown woman, employed in the greatest house in Glamorganshire. I expect that Master Eyes told the Cook that I can read and write, so I expect I shall be my Mistress's helper in some way. Now I am even more glad of all those days with Dada and Mam, scratching like a chicken on that old slate, even when the sun was warm outside and I longed to run about, because otherwise I might have to be a scullery maid. Would anything be more horrible than to spend my days up to my armpits in cold, greasy water?

And then we arrived! Wil-bach reined in old Mari outside some wide iron gates, and there was Llancaiach Fawr. The house is *huge*, bigger than any house I have ever seen, except Cardiff Castle, which I saw once, which does not count, of course, being a castle.

Llancaiach is built of a mellow stone that is almost the colour of honey, and there are too many windows to count, because my hands are in mittens and my feet in boots and I get muddled after ten since I can read much better than I can count. There is a beautiful garden – or it will be, I expect, when it is summer and there are flowers. And such a grand entrance, the doorway with a pointed arch shut tight against the cold January air.

Mari tossed her head, snuffling and snorting, her breath steaming as Wil climbed down.

'*Nawr te, cariad fach,*'[7] he said, hauling down my bundle, 'you mind and be a good girl. Work hard

---

[7] Now then, little sweetheart

13

and make your Mam and your Dada, *heddwch i'w lwch,*[8] proud, is it?'

I gave the old man a hug and tried not to cry. He looked up at the grey-yellow winter sky, and frowned. 'Better perhaps I stay overnight in Bedlinog, where my cousin has a little house, and go back tomorrow. Give your love to your Mam, shall I?' He climbed back up to his perch on the cart, wiped the dew-drop off his nose with his sleeve and winked at me.

'I shall see you on your day off, lovely girl,' he said, and slapped Mari with the reins. 'Get word to your Mam when it will be, and I shall come and wait for you if I can.'

When Mari had clopped around the bend in the road, I set off down the path. At the door, I clutched my bundle to my chest, and quaked. It was even grander close up, and heavier, and taking a deep breath, I lifted the great iron ring and clattered it down.

---

[8] Rest in peace

My Journal:

Well, Mam, Here I am at Llancaiach Fawr and a fine House it is. All the Servants are friendly and I am Sure I shall not be Homesick at all, although of course I shall Miss you. The gardens are Beautiful even all frosted with Winter. I shall Write about the Inside when I have seen More of it.

Author's note:

You may notice that Tirion's spelling is very good. That's because I've corrected it to make it easy for you to understand. In her time, everyone's spelling, even that of important people, was very, very bad. Everyone spelled phonetically – that is, they wrote down what they heard, and they put capital letters wherever they fancied, so Tirion's Journal for her Mam might have read:

> *Wel, Mam, Heer I Am at Llancaiach Fawr – and a Fyne Howse it is. Alle the Servants are frendily and I amme Sewer I shal not be Homsicke at alle, althow of corse I shal Mis you. The gardyns are Buteyfull even all frosted with Winter. I shal Rite abowt the Insyde when I have seen Moore of it.*

Chapter Two

However, the door stayed very tightly shut, and I had to put down my bundle and bash again, very hard on the thick wood. The January wind cut like a knife through my wool cloak, and by the time the inner door was opened, and then the outer door unbolted,[1] my teeth were chattering and my feet were numb.

A tall man peered down his nose at me.

'What do you want, girl?' he asked in Welsh.

'If you please, sir, I am Tirion Griffiths, and I have come to work here.'

He sniffed. 'Wait there.' He turned and walked away, his shoe heels rapping loudly on the wooden floor.

After a little while, by which time my nose had almost frozen solid, a short lady, not much taller than me, wearing a neat grey dress and spotless white cap and apron appeared. Her eyes crinkled in a friendly way, and her smile, when it came, was

---

[1] There were two doors to every room to keep the warmth in – and between Colonel Prichard's chamber and the next room were three, to keep his secrets from being overheard!

welcoming. I dropped a curtsey, despite my bundle. My Mam taught me manners.

'Oh, Tirion, is it?' she asked,[2] reaching out a hand to tug me inside. 'Come you in, child. You must be frozen, travelling all this way on such a bitter old day.' She shut both the doors, to keep the cold out, and guided me into the house.

I barely had time to goggle at the grand staircase, before being ushered down a passageway and into a kitchen bustling with people.

In the middle of the room, like a black-beetle in a pan of milk, stood a boy. He was filthier than any person I had ever seen before in my whole life. He was black from head to toe, his blue eyes gleaming in the middle of a coal-black face, his open mouth bright red in contrast, like a coal-miner. I stared at him, and he stopped coughing, pulled a face and stuck out his tongue, which looked like a fat red worm coming out of the blackness.

I did not stick out my tongue, although I wanted to. After all, I am a grown woman now, and taking up my first position in life, and such behaviour is beneath me.

---

[2] Downstairs, the servants all spoke Welsh, but Colonel Prichard and his wife spoke English because they were proud that they had mastered it – although of course they could speak Welsh too.

'Take no notice of Ifor. He is only the spit-boy[3] and has not the sense he was born with, to stand beneath a chimney looking up, when it is being swept.' She shook her head, pityingly. '*Twp*, he is!'

'First time I did ever see the chimney swept. I wanted to see the holly bush come down,' the boy muttered. 'Didn't think it would come that quick, did I?'

The woman shook her head. 'Addled as an egg, you! Not the bush you should look out for, *boi bach*, but the soot! Tirion, I am Catrin, maid of all work. The black boy here is not Prince Charles,[4] but only Ifor ap Iestyn, spit-boy and village idiot.'

The room was large and whitewashed, filled with wooden tables and benches. Each side of the fire hung a rack filled with horn and wooden spoons – one belonging to each servant. I had brought my

---

[3] Spit-boy doesn't mean he went around spitting at people. There were no gas or electric ovens, so joints of meat had an iron rod stuck through them and they were put on a rack close to the open kitchen fire to cook. It was Ifor's job to sit and turn the handle so the meat rotated and wouldn't burn. In earlier times, there was often a little dog in a tread-mill cage who was prodded so that he ran, which made the spit wheel turn!

[4] When Prince Charles (later Charles II) was born, he was so dark-skinned and dark-haired (and he was also rather ugly!) that his mother, Queen Henrietta Maria, called him her 'Black Boy'. He earned some much ruder nicknames later in life!

own spoon that Wil-bach had made for me from the horn of his best cow when she died, with my initials, TG, and my year of birth, 1635, carved on it. Wil can't read or write, but my Dada had written it down for him and he had copied it, although he had carved the '3' backwards.

Barrels and baskets stood against the walls, covered with sacking against the soot, and dried herbs and joints of bacon hung from hooks. There should have been a fire blazing in the hearth, but instead there was a heap of soot and a large holly bush on a piece of string.

'Bleddyn Cook coughed so hard cooking dinner yesterday he said we must sweep the chimneys, the Lord's Day or not. "No more cooking until it is done," he said.' Catrin shook her head. 'And now, thanks to this one here, we have a fine mess to clear up. Still, he made it, he can clean it. Go and wash, Ifor, as soon as you have cleaned up the soot.'

She turned to me. 'Put your things down, Tirion. It is nearly supper time, and –' she grabbed my hand and rubbed it vigorously – 'there, you are frozen. Come with me, and I will find you a nice warm drink.'

She led me through the kitchen into a large room lined with tables. A spinning wheel stood beside the fireplace, which had only recently been re-lighted from the look of it. Perhaps both fires shared the one chimney and both had to be put out to sweep it. I held my hands out to it for warmth, and looked around.

The people in there were all busy, one dipping candles, one stitching away at a piece of white cloth, another pounding something with a pestle in a mortar.

A young girl glanced up, smiling. 'This is Rachel Edmund,' Catrin said, 'who is a maid of all work like me. Here is Tirion, who has come to join us. Tirion, this is Enid Samuel, who knows more about cows and horses than any man you will ever meet. Enid, Bleddyn Cook is shouting for butter. He is in a terrible temper because of the mess in the kitchen, but it was he who wanted the chimney swept, and in January too, and so he must put up with it.'

'Always short-tempered, that one,' Enid said, but she was smiling as she said it. 'Must be the heat in the kitchen – except that he's let the fire go out and now he has to get it lighted again in time to cook supper, or use our fire in here. Good thing the family is having only bread and broth, isn't it?'

I scowled. Not at Catrin, I liked her, but at the boy, who was pulling hideous faces at me over her shoulder.

'You!' Catrin turned and pointed at filthy Ifor. 'Have you cleaned up that soot yet?'

Ifor shook his grimy head, and showers of black snow scattered round him. 'No, Catrin. Hannah Saer and Siani Thomas are doing it. Hannah said I was making a bigger mess cleaning it up than it was before. I tried to wash it up instead of sweeping it, and it all went to mud.'

I think he'd been crying. There were two clean tracks running from his eyes to his chin and he was sniffing.

'Then what are you doing loitering around by here? Go and wash yourself under the stable-yard pump,[5] and come back when you are clean again.'

'But it's bitter outside, Catrin!' he protested.

'Your fault for being stupid. Get on with you. Go on, go!'

Ifor slouched off, muttering.

'And I shall look behind your ears when you come back, so make sure you remember to scrub them!'

---

[5] There was no running water inside the house. It was brought from outside in buckets, every drop, from a pump or a well, but there were handy little sluices in the kitchen walls so the dirty water could be chucked away easily.

Enid came back. 'Take off that good cloak, Tirion – there's a lovely name for a girl, isn't it, Catrin? *Gentle*, it means. Are you gentle, Tirion?'

'I try to be,' I said, shyly. 'But I'm a bit clumsy, as well.'

'Well, I am sure you will fit in well here, then,' Catrin chuckled. 'For I am clumsy as an ox in an alehouse, and that's the truth.'

'What do you know about alehouses?' Enid asked, pretending to be shocked. 'Nothing at all, I hope!'

'Oh, before I forget!' Catrin said suddenly. 'The Mistress was complaining that there is no dry moss in the House of Commons – hard to get it dry this time of year, no wonder, is it?' Catrin tutted to herself.

I wondered why the House of Commons should need dry moss – and what it had to do with Llancaiach Fawr – but I expect I shall find out. Perhaps it is a new sort of Tax on rich people, although taxes are usually money.

I must make sure I don't show my ignorance by having to ask. Listen and learn, that's my motto – and only ask questions if I can't find out any other way!

Ifor the spit-boy came back, was inspected – especially behind the ears and around the neck – and sent back to wash again. This time he was told to change his clothes, too, the ones he was wearing being thick with soot.

'But I only got my Sunday best, Catrin! I can't wear my Sunday best to clean the pots. They will get ruined!'

'I could lend you a dress to wear,' Catrin said. 'You would look pretty in a dress, Ifor.'

'O, cau dy geg,'[6] the boy muttered, and was clipped smartly round the ear for being cheeky. I almost felt sorry for him. Almost.

'Come and see me when you are clean,' Enid instructed. 'I shall find you clothes to wear – there are usually old breeches hanging about in the stable. They will smell of horse, and you are so skinny they will likely fall off you, but better that than spoil good clothes.'

Ifor wandered off miserably to wash again, and Enid, wrapping her shawl around her against the freezing weather, went off to the stables.

Catrin turned to me. 'No work for you tonight, Tirion. You must be tired out from your journey, and anyway there is very little to do, because it is Sunday. The family eats a large dinner, but supper is

---

[6] Shut your mouth

only light, and Sunday night we are all allowed to rest after the week. You will start tomorrow, Plough Monday, and don't worry. I shall help you until you get used to it.'

Here was my chance to find out my duties. 'Shall I be a chambermaid?'

'Bless you, no! Two chambermaids already, Esther Griffiths and Sarah Parry, who is the Mistress's maid, and I am the maid of all work, doing a bit of everything, going where I am needed. No, Tirion, you will be helping me.'

My heart sank. I should have known that Master Eyes and Ears would not tell them I could read, and so I was only going to be a maid of all work. Still, that was better than being a scullery maid. I hate washing pots – I'd done enough of that at home. Perhaps Colonel Pritchard might find out that I can read and write, and one day he may give me a better job.

'But the most important part of your work – the Mistress has asked especially –'

This was better. Mistress Pritchard had asked specially! Important job! I could bear being a maid of all work if I had an *important* job, too.

'– a job your stepfather said you would be especially good at –'

I beamed, feeling better all the time.

'– a job that will take you all over the house, from top to bottom, even in the Master and the Mistress's chambers and the Steward's office, which is an honour not given to many of us, who have our own places and must stay in them –'

Better still! I thought gleefully.

'– because dear Nan Bedlinog, who used to be the Master's nurse when he was a little boy, is too old to do it now –'

Really important, then, I thought. Old nurses were always respected.

'– you, Tirion, are going to be the spider-brusher!'

Aaaaaaargh!

My Journal

Well, Mam, I must say that anyone would appreciate my dear Stepfather's kindness in speaking of me to Master Bleddyn ap Thomas the Cook here at Llancaiach. He has ensured that I have a Position within the Household that will earn me some respect and also a Good Living so that I can send Money home to Help.

Do not worry about me, Mam. I miss you already but I know that I am very Lucky to have been found such good, steady Work when I am only a girl.

Please tell my Dear Stepfather that I am most grateful for his Speaking for me, and that one day I Hope to Repay him in Full . . .

Chapter Three

I want to go home! A spider-brusher! Oh, I want to repay my stepfather all right! I want to squeeze his scrawny throat until his eyes pop out. I want to kick his shins and bite his ankles and stick pins in him until he squeals. He knows perfectly well that the thing that terrifies me most in the whole world, after the Plague, is spiders.

I hate their eight long, black, scary legs.

I hate the way they can hide themselves so that you can't see them until they move.

I hate the way they make webs so that you walk into them with your face and they stick.

Spiders make me feel sick and shaky and so scared I can't even run. I just freeze. Sometimes I scream, but not since Mam married Old Eyes and Ears, because if I do, his horrible son will pick the spider up and chase me with it. Once he put one down my neck and I fainted. But when I came to, I was sick on him, which made me feel better. Mam scolded him, but his father said he was only having fun. Fun? Not to me it wasn't.

27

So this is Master Eyes and Ears' revenge. Just because I bit him when he beat me. A little devil tempted me, I swear, and for once I fought back. His fat, freckly arm was there, and I stretched my neck and bared my teeth and bit him. Hard. He yelled and let go of me, and I ran and hid. He beat me some more, later, but it made me feel better to see the bandage tied round his arm. I'd do it again, I would, so there.

But he has had the last laugh, hasn't he? He's got me a job as a spider-brusher.

Catrin stared at me. 'What's the matter, Tirion? You've gone white as a sheet! Are you ill?'

I shook my head, numbly. How could I admit that I couldn't do the very job I'd been hired to do? 'But Catrin, I can read and write,' I blurted. 'Isn't there something better I could do instead?'

Catrin's face changed from friendly in an instant. 'Oh, *Diawl*,[1] not another one! That Hannah Saer keeps boasting she can read, too.' She wagged her finger at me. 'Don't tell lies, Tirion. Your sins will find you out, and if Mrs Thomas the Housekeeper hears you, she will be angry. Girls can't read and write, not girls like you, anyway, so don't go saying

---

[1] Devil

you can. Do you think you are too good, perhaps, to do a job like me?'

'But –' I stammered.

'But me no buts! Look, I will show you where you will sleep and you can bring your things up now.' She was cross with me, I could see it in her face – but I was telling the truth! It wasn't fair.

Catrin stamped up the back stairs, up and up and up. On the next landing she found a candle, struck tinder to light it, and we mounted the last flight of steep, twisting stairs, the shadows leaping around like ghosts. Or spiders, I thought, glumly. There were probably countless spiders up here beneath the roof. Waiting . . .

She pushed open a low door. 'Women in here, men over by there,' she said, indicating another door. I followed her in, out of breath and hugging my bundle.

The floor was loose planks laid across the ceiling joists so that people would not fall through the lath-and-plaster into the rooms below, and the roof sloped right down to the floor at the edges. The square chimney breast rose up through the floor on its way out of the roof. Heaps of straw, one or two rough mattresses made of sacking and rough blankets served as beds. I had a cupboard bed[2] at home, with doors I could shut to keep out the draught and prying eyes. But here I would sleep with all the other women who lived-in. I took a deep breath. Something else that was new! Something scrabbled behind me. I turned to look and a mouse scuttled into a hole in the corner. I hoped there were not rats, too. I do not like rats.

I dropped my bundle well away from the mouse-hole, near the chimney wall. 'I'll put my stuff here, shall I?' I said, thinking that I should at least be warm even if I shouldn't be comfortable.

'Indeed you will not!' Catrin said, still cross. 'You need to learn your place, my girl, and quick. Your elders and betters[3] sleep close to the chimneys where it is warm. You will sleep there,' she said, indicating a place under the eaves. I picked up my bundle and put it where she pointed. An icicle had formed just about where my nose would be when I was lying down.

Tears prickled in my eyes, and I felt about as miserable as it is possible for a person to be. I sniffled.

---

[2] You may have seen one of these at St Fagan's Welsh Folk Museum: it is a bed, usually downstairs, that is built into the wall like a cupboard, with doors. Imagine how dark and stuffy that must have been! But possibly better than an attic with bare floors and maybe rats . . .

[3] Anyone among the women servants who was older or in a better job than Tirion. That is, everyone!

At the sound, Catrin lifted the candle. Her cross face disappeared. 'What? Are you crying? Oh, *cariad*, you are homesick, is it? Far away from home, first time away from your Mammy. There, there now. I didn't mean to be cross with you. But you shouldn't go about saying you can do things that you can't, you know. It will only get you in trouble, and it makes people cross.'

She opened her arms and wrapped them round me, hugging me hard. 'I didn't mean to be nasty, honest I didn't. Look, come downstairs and we'll have something warm to drink.'

I wanted to tell her that it wasn't homesickness – well, not yet, anyway, even if I did want my Mam.

It was just the thought of spending my life actually *looking* for spiders instead of running in the opposite direction. Couldn't tell her that, though, could I? Lose my job in a minute, then. Sniffing, for I had lost the bit of rag Mam gave me for a kerchief,[4] I followed her downstairs.

Back in the servants' hall, Ifor the sooty boy was sitting at the table getting his face into a thickly-buttered piece of crusty bread. He looked up and grinned. It wasn't a nice grin, even now that his face was cleaner. I think he was about my own age, or

---

[4] And that was posh, too. Most people used their sleeves . . .

maybe eleven or twelve. It was hard to tell, because he was so skinny and scrawny.

'Your ugly old face is like a slapped backside,' he said, and a fair-haired lady in a neat grey gown clipped him smartly round the ear. He seemed to get his ear smacked quite a lot, our Ifor. Good. Save me doing it for him. He deserved whatever he got.

'Mind your language, Ifor ap Iestyn!' the lady said sternly. 'The child has only just arrived, and you will be kind to her. And I remember you snivelling and wailing for your Mam when you came by here first, so don't you put on airs!'

Catrin chuckled. 'Aye, that's true. Wept buckets, he did! Tirion, this kind lady here is Sarah Parry, maid to Colonel Prichard's wife. The Mistress has two little girls, Jane and Mary. Jane is twelve, older than you, almost grown-up, but little Mary is only three, and full of mischief. Many a berating does she get, and many a loving beating too, but there is no harm in her.'

Sarah Parry, her fair hair tucked neatly beneath a white cap, smiled. 'Tirion, is it? Lovely name, that – "gentle". Are you gentle, Tirion?'

Ifor sniggered and opened his mouth, probably to say something clever, but I have a tongue in my head, and I am not afraid to use it.

'I am mostly as gentle as I can possibly be,' I said smartly, 'but if anyone –' I glared at Ifor – 'if anyone upsets me, then I can be very, very rough, too!'

Sarah hid a grin, and Catrin laughed out loud. 'Good for you, Tirion. Keep this little limb of Satan in his place. Someone needs to. And if you've finished feeding your face, young Ifor, I'm sure Bleddyn Cook has something you can usefully do. Better you go before he shouts – always better that way, and you know he's going to shout anyw –'

'Ifor!' a voice bellowed. 'Where is that boy? He's never here when I want him. Iiiiiiifoooor!'

Ifor was out from behind the table and gone in an instant, bread and butter forgotten.

'If that boy moved as fast about his duties as he does when he's about to get in trouble, he'd be promoted to stable boy tomorrow,' Enid Samuel chuckled. 'He knows what end of a horse is what, and more besides.'

'Don't let him hear you say that, Enid,' Catrin warned, 'bad enough already, that one, always going on about his stupid old horses. Now, Tirion, sit here by the fire. Off duty, now, nearly all of us, so you can meet everybody and drink some warmed ale.'[5]

---

5 Everyone drank ale, even children.

My Journal

Well, Mam, I have met some of the other Servants here. They are mostly very Kind but there is a boy who is Rude and Unpleasant, and to my Mind should have been beaten often when he was much smaller. I shall pray for him to be a better boy.*

I have not met the Family yet, but as well as Colonel Prichard and his Wife, there are two daughters, Jane who is twelve and Mary who is three. Catrin Howell, who is maid of all work, is very kind and she will show me my duties. Catrin said that the Master also Once had two Sons called Thomas and Lewis, but they died when they were babies, which is very sad. But then of course, my own dear Brothers and Sister also died when they were but Infants. I am happy that God Spared me to take up my present Station in Life.

---

* I shall pray for him, but I shall also smack him very hard if he annoys me any more.

The Mistress is collecting dried moss for the House of Commons. I do not know what the House of Commons will use it for, but I expect you will, because you know everything, Mam. I cannot understand it too well, because Colonel Prichard is for the King, and I cannot understand why his wife would want to give anything to the Parliamentarians, even if it is only moss.

Author's note:

It was usual for a mother to have seven or eight or even more children than that, and for all but one or two to die as babies. There were no antibiotics to get them over such small things as earaches and sore throats, and so they often died of simple things that would be cured very quickly today.

Chapter Four

I sat on a low stool beside the fire, sipping warmed ale sweetened with honey and feeling as miserable and homesick as I have ever felt. One by one they came in: Elisabeth Proude, the Mistress's seamstress, Hannah Saer, the laundry-maid, and even Master Bolitho, Colonel Prichard's valet, who was so important that he even slept in the Master's chamber, on a pull-out truckle bed.[1] Catrin whispered to me as each person came in, telling me who they were. To some, she introduced me, to others she did not, me being too lowly for them to bother with.

Bleddyn ap Thomas, the Cook, came through from the kitchens, his face red from the fires, which were now blazing.

Unlike Master Bolitho, who did not seem even to see me, Master Thomas peered down his expanse of

---

[1] That is, it was pulled out from under Colonel Prichard's bed every night and the Colonel's valet slept on the floor beside him in case the Master needed anything in the night. And in the morning it was shoved back under the bed again. The lower the bed, the lower the servant – which is why Tirion sleeps on the floor!

brown-clad belly at me. My Mam used to say that a skinny cook was no good to man nor beast. Bleddyn Cook would not have disappointed her, for his stomach was as round and comfortable as a cushion, and he looked like one of the big, brown bears that danced in the street on market day.[2]

'What have we here?' he boomed.

I opened my mouth to say, 'I am a who, not a what,' but a nudge from Catrin on one side and Enid Samuel on the other shut me up. I'd been brought up to speak when I was spoken to, and I had been spoken to. But here, it seemed, I had to let others answer for me.

'This is our new spider-brusher,' Enid Samuel introduced me. 'Tirion Griffiths.'

'Tirion, is it?' Bleddyn Cook roared, 'and are you gentle, Tirion?'

I smiled and lowered my eyes and tried to look gentle, but if everyone was going to make the same joke, I was going to get fed up very quickly.

'Well, *croeso i* Lancaiach Fawr,[3] child. Your

---

[2] Bears were caught, their claws and teeth pulled out or blunted, and made to 'dance' by being prodded with a sharp stick. There are laws against such dreadful cruelty now, but there was no RSPCA to look after animals in those days.

[3] Welcome to.

stepfather has told me that you are a hard worker but that you can be insolent and disobedient, too. Well, we shall forget all that. I speak as I find, and if you work hard you will be happy here. Mind you, if you don't work hard, you will have Hannah Saer after you, for she is death to slackers.'

I was nudged again, and I took it that now I was allowed to speak. 'I promise I'll work hard, Master Bleddyn,' I vowed. And I would, I would – if only there were no spiders. I looked around, fearfully, at the whitewashed walls of the Servants' Hall. A house this size might have millions!

Another girl, slim and dark, bits of straw clinging to her skirt, came into the room, brushing snow off her cloak. 'The weather has turned worse. I knew it would,' she said glumly. 'We shall all be snowed in and I shall not get home to see my Mam next Sunday. Too far to walk when there's snow, even if it is only five miles each way.'

'Perhaps it will be all gone by then, Siani,' Catrin comforted her. 'Come and get warm by the fire, now. Here is Tirion, who has come to help us in the house – she will be Spider-brusher now, Siani, instead of you!'

Siani smiled. She unfastened her cloak and hung it on a peg. 'That's good. Now I can get back to my geese, instead of making beds and rushing about the house after spiders. There's a thing, the Mistress being so afraid of little old things like that. But Tirion, the minute she sees one, off goes the bell, as if Old Scratch[4] himself was after her, clang, clang, and then I must rush to catch the thing and kill it. Don't know why I have to kill it, mind, because to my way of thinking, spiders are not so bad. They catch flies in summer, and I'd rather have a spider than a nasty, buzzing old fly, any old day.'

'Are there lots of spiders?' I asked, my voice creaking a bit.

'Not down by here,' Enid Samuel replied, 'because Mrs Ann Thomas Housekeeper is death on spiders. But since the Master had the upstairs wood-panelled, well, they seem to be everywhere. Don't show up, on panelling, not like on nice, clean whitewash, and so the housemaids don't see them unless they move, and there are so many little tiny ledges in the wood where they can sit and spin their old webs. This time of year, there are dozens of them. I think they come inside out of the cold!'

I gulped.

'The Mistress had a blue fit yesterday,' Siani said,

---

4 The Devil (again!)

grinning. 'The bells were clanging like ten churches on a Sunday, and she was shrieking and standing on a chair, waving her arms as if she'd run lunatical. Mind, it was a big one. Legs like one of Elisabeth's sewing needles, and its body – well, as big as a plum, it was, honest!'

I thought I might faint. Could I run away without anyone seeing me? Where could I go if I did? Siani said it was snowing outside. I couldn't go anywhere, not in snow. I'd die of cold before I went a mile. And it was a lot more than a mile back home, because it took nearly a whole day to get here, even by Wilbach's horse and cart. And if I went home, Old Eyes and Ears would only beat me and send me back, so what was the use?

I noticed the spit-boy watching me, and tried to look calm and happy. I felt that if I showed any sign of weakness, he would strike like the nasty little weasel he was.

When Mrs Ann Thomas, the housekeeper, whose word was law below stairs, came into the Servants' Hall, she frowned at me, although I had an odd feeling that perhaps she wasn't quite as stern as she tried to appear. She reminded me a bit of my Mam, with the same dark eyebrows and calm eyes.

'*Nawr te*, Tirion,' she said. 'Although your place in

the House is a lowly one, you are in a special position. You have been taken on by the finest, kindest, fairest gentleman in three counties, and you will be trusted to go anywhere at all in the house, which very few of the other servants may. You must go each day into every room – first knocking and asking permission to make sure it is all right for you to enter, of course – and quietly and quickly you must get rid of every web and every spider that you can see.'

If I keep my eyes shut, maybe I won't see any at all . . . I thought. *But then, they will still be able to see me, won't they?*

'And if you miss any, be certain the Mistress will call you back, and then there will be trouble. Pay special attention to the Mistress's bedchamber, and the Great Hall, the Still Room where she makes her cordials, anywhere the Mistress is likely to go. And don't forget the Commons. *Diawl,* I tell you, there was a spider in the Commons only a week ago that could have carried off Miss Mary with no trouble at all.'

I must have looked puzzled. What would Miss Mary be doing in the House of Commons?

Hannah Saer giggled. 'You don't know what Mrs Ann means, do you, Tirion?'

I shook my head, feeling stupid and ignorant.

'The bog. The loo. The privy. The jakes!'

The Housekeeper scowled. 'Vulgar, vulgar, Hannah! I will not put up with that.' She turned her attention back to me. 'In this house, the commons, the jakes – garderobes, if you wish,' she said, frowning at Hannah again, 'whatever you might call the place the gentry go to do their – er – business, are inside the house. There are four, one in the Withdrawing Room, where the family sits, and another upstairs, although they do not connect at all, so there is no danger to the gentry from sitting there. Catrin will show you in the morning when she takes you around the house. You may not, of course, use them. Elisabeth Proude has permission to use the upstairs privy, but she does not like it. She says it is much too draughty!'

'All the same,' Catrin said, 'draughty or not I expect it's warmer than going to the jakes at the bottom of the garden and hanging our bums over the stream like we have to. Freeze your –'

'Catrin!' the Housekeeper said, sharply. 'Enough.'

'When you have made sure,' she went on, turning back to me, 'that all the spiders are gone, then you will report to Master Bleddyn the Cook, or to Catrin, or to me, for other duties. Do you understand?'

I nodded, miserably. 'If you please?' I began.

Mrs Ann, Housekeeper, raised an eyebrow at me. 'Yes?'

'Do I have to do the spiders *every* day?'

'Twice a day,' she said, implacably. 'Except on your day off, which will be the last Sunday every month – unless you are needed here, of course.'

'Oh.' No escape there, then.

Bleddyn Cook was watching me. 'Is something wrong, Tirion?'

'No, sir,' I lied.

'Are you sure? Your stepfather said you were a hard-working girl. I would not have spoken to Master Mathias for you, otherwise.'

'I do work hard,' I said glumly. 'Ever so hard. But –'

Ifor the spit-boy was watching me. 'I know,' he said, wickedly. 'She's afeard of spiders. You are, aren't you?'

I said it before I could stop myself. 'I am not!' I said, loudly. 'If I see a spider, I squash it flat, so there.' *Just like I'll squash you, you horrible boy, you, if you try to get me in trouble again!* I thought. Behind Mrs Ann's back I pulled my best cross-eyed face. He pulled one back, but was seen and got his ear clouted again, which made me feel better.

Didn't change anything, though. My Mam always says, when you are stuck with a thing, you might as well make the best of it. Actually, she used to say 'What can't be cured must be endured,' which is the same thing.

So I was stuck, it seemed, with making the best of spiders.

My Journal

Well, Mam, I have met Master Bleddyn ap Thomas, Stepfather's* Friend, who is just as you always say a cook should be - he is quite Round. He seems Kind but Stern. He was Anxious that all my Stepfather told him about me was true. I assured him that it was, and I Vow I shall do my best to prove Worthy of You, Mam, and Behave as a Good girl should, and work Hard.

As for my Work here, the Master and Mistress do not Know that I am able to Read and Write a little, and so my daily Round is not quite what I expected. But I am Sure I shall do as well as you would wish me to.**

---

* Whom I have Not Forgotten. I shall seek my Vengeance. Some slow and painful death, with deadly poison snakes, perhaps.
** If I do not die from terror first.

Chapter Five

It was the coldest, most miserable night I have ever spent. I snivelled a lot from homesickness and misery. My mattress of musty straw didn't do anything to cushion my bony hips from the wooden floor, and when my breath warmed the icicle above my nose, it melted and dripped (the icicle, not my nose) down my neck. My feet, despite the rough blanket and my good wool cloak that I had pulled over me for extra warmth, were like two blocks of ice. I don't think I slept at all, but I must have, because I dreamed of spiders. Giant spiders, the size of plough horses, towering over me clashing their fangs and waving their horrid legs.

When Sarah Parry, with her candle flickering in the darkness, shook me awake, there was not even a hint of dawn and my eyes felt sore and gritty from tiredness. It was pitch-black in the attic except for the little candlelight, and all around me I could see the dim shapes of the other women moving about. Sarah handed me a bundle of clothes and told me to come downstairs when I was dressed. I put them on by the flicker of the candlelight: a grey woollen dress, white cap and pinafore. Glad of the thick clothes and warmth, I crept out of the attic, stuffing my long plaits up under the cap.

I closed the door softly behind me, and felt my way in the semi-darkness towards the top of the stairs. The candle had been left on the next landing down, and as I reached the top step – something crawled on my neck!

'Aaaagh!' I screamed, and leapt forward. I crashed down the stairs and landed hard on my bum. I frantically brushed at my face, neck, my hair, half-hysterical[1] with fright.

'Knew you were afraid of spiders!' Ifor whispered in my ear, pushing past me down the stairs. I glared after him. One day, I will kill him. Painfully, perhaps with red hot pincers in it somewhere . . .

All around me people were waking up – crossly – for not all the servants' days began as early as mine and Sarah's, and I decided it would be a good idea to disappear before they discovered who had made all the row and woken them.

---

[1] Just as well Tirion didn't have *whole* hysterics: the treatment for *that* was to be bled. Her vein would have been opened and half a pint or so of blood let out until she stopped shrieking . . .

I crept, aching, shaking, homesick and tearful down to the kitchen, where I was given some hot porridge that had been sitting on the fire-hob all night to cook, with salt and creamy milk from the dairy. Honey to sweeten it would have been better, but Hannah Saer refused to give me any, for fear of the tooth-worm.[2] Hannah is sure the tooth-worm feeds on sugar and sweetness. I wanted to say that they were my teeth, let me have honey, but I was too miserable to bother.

Ifor sat in the corner grinning, shovelling porridge into his mouth. He had honey on his, which he had taken from the crock when Hannah wasn't looking. He made a creepy-crawly movement with his fingers in the air.

You wait, boy, I thought, *I will have you for that, one day.* I remembered the Scriptures that Dada read to

---

[2] An abscess on the tooth, and toothache, were thought to be caused by a burrowing toothworm. Without antibiotics, a tooth abscess could kill a person then. Dental care was awful – a book called *'The Queen's Closet Open'd'* published in the 17th Century advised washing the mouth every morning with lemon juice, then rubbing your teeth with a sage leaf, and rinsing with water after eating meat – no toothbrushes. Mind, if your teeth fell – or were pulled out, with no anaesthetic – you could always buy animal teeth or some other, possibly dead, person's left over teeth, and have them fitted, instead . . .

me: Vengeance is Mine, Saith the Lord – but if you want my opinion, God moves too slow for my taste, and I don't think I can wait for the Last Trump before seeing both Ifor and my stepfather suffer for their misdeeds.

I was grateful for the warmth of the kitchen, and wished that I could stay there, full up with hot porridge, but as soon as I had finished eating, my training began. Sarah showed me how she prepared her Mistress's breakfast tray.

'If it should be my day off, and if for some reason Catrin should not be here, then it will be your task, perhaps, to do this some day, so it is as well you know. I have to heat water on the fire and carry it upstairs for the Mistress to wash her face and hands. You can carry the jug upstairs for me when it is ready. For breakfast, the Mistress will have cheese, spiced meats and claret wine,[3] and she will have it sharp at six, for she doesn't like to lie abed.' Sarah picked up a small bottle and slipped it into her apron pocket.

'What's that?' I asked, curious.

'Well, there is a new baby in the village, and as soon as I heard about it, I sent one of the under-

---

[3] NOBODY drank water – unless they wanted to die a horrible death from sickness and diarrhoea. It wasn't clean enough!

maids to visit and collect its, its, –' she looked vaguely embarrassed, 'its wee.'

I stared at her. 'What on earth for?'

'It is easy to see that you are a country girl, Tirion,' Sarah said, smiling. 'For everyone knows that a new-born baby's wee is the best thing in all the world for the complexion. The Mistress swears by it, and she has scarcely a wrinkle, despite her age.'

I decided I would rather have wrinkles than wash my face in wee!

'The Mistress,' Sarah went on, 'is a fine lady who knows how to keep her beauty, even though she is quite old. She rubs white lead into her cheeks to make her complexion pale, and uses charcoal to darken her eyebrows. Do you know,' she said pulling a face, 'that in London, the fine ladies shave off their eyebrows, and stick on new ones cut from mouse-skin! And they make patterns of moons and stars, and stick those on, too. I heard tell that one lady had a coach and horses, all cut out of mouse-skin, running across her face!' She shuddered. 'I do not like mice, and I would rather not be beautiful than have their skin stuck to me anywhere. Ugh!'

I agreed. *Dim diolch*![4]

---

[4] No thanks!

'Mind you,' Sarah chattered on, 'that is London for you. They say it is a terrible place. Dirty and smelly and smoky and noisy, and everybody throws what's in their chamber pots straight out of the upstairs windows,[5] which is disgusting, to my mind.[6] Don't find decent Welsh people doing that, do you? All the same,' she said, wistfully. 'I should like to go and see it, one day. Perhaps when the war is over.'

The Mistress's breakfast ready, Sarah picked up the tray and I followed her up the stairs. Sarah rapped on the door and then entered the bed-chamber. The jug of hot water was heavy, and it was all I could do to carry it without slopping the hot water over myself. I was glad to be able to put it down on the table beside the wash basin. I stood, my hands clasped meekly in front of me, my eyes (which probably should have been lowered respectfully) everywhere. I was too nosy to be respectful, that first morning!

When Sarah lit the candles and drew back the

---

[5] They would chuck it out and – sometimes – shout 'Gardy loo!' – or *'Gardez l'eau'* ('look out for the water' in French) and everybody had to jump out of the way, quick. That's where our word for toilet – loo – comes from.

[6] Sarah was right, London was disgusting – everybody chucked everything out of their windows – rotten food, paper, floor sweepings, ashes, as well as poo and wee, and every so often rickety carts would come round to clear it, and drive away with the rubbish spilling everywhere.

bed-curtains, the lady woke and stretched, yawning, leaning forward while Sarah plumped the pillows to help her sit up. Sarah signalled to me to light the other candles on the bedside table and on the window sill, placed the tray on Mistress Prichard's lap and curtseyed, folding her hands and waiting.

The Mistress was not old, but neither was she young, and I think perhaps she had once been very pretty, although there were little lines and wrinkles on her forehead and around her eyes, so the new-born baby's wee didn't work all that well, did it? She picked up her beaker of wine and took a sip, her eyes still closed.

I sneaked looks around me. On the window sill beside the candle were bowls of dried flowers, and bottles and jars labelled in neat black writing – feverfew, rosemary, agrimony, chamomile and motherwort. All the herbs were familiar to me from my own Mam's still-room, and I noticed dried lavender as well, to make the room smell sweet and keep disease away.[7]

---

[7] In time of plague, people would carry little bunches of fragrant flowers to sniff, because they believed that the plague was airborne, and having something to smell would keep the plague away. Of course it didn't – we know now that the plague was carried by fleas that jumped off the bodies of dead

Sarah took the little bottle from her apron pocket and set it on the table.

'Excellent,' the lady said, opening her eyes. 'And who is this, Sarah?'

'If you please, Ma'am, this is Tirion Griffiths, who is here to help us.'

The lady looked at me. 'I hope you are a good girl, Tirion, and that you will work hard. We have only hard workers here at Llancaiach. And you must be quiet, especially when I have a headache. I cannot bear noise about me.'

'No, Mistress,' I mumbled. Sarah nudged me, and I understood quickly that here, too, I was not expected to speak even when I was spoken to, just bob up and down silently.

'Sarah, send Proude to me, if you will. There is a rip in my second-best gown, although I do not remember tearing it. And lay out the second-best lace-edged collar to go with my dress: the other is grimy and needs laundering. I think I shall wear the thicker bum-roll today – the padding will help keep me warm.'[8]

---

black rats onto human beings, and bit them, giving them the disease . . .

[8] There. Told you bum was a perfectly good word, didn't I? Mistress Prichard's bum-roll was worn around her bum to make her hips look bigger – a bit different to today, when ladies all want their bums to look small!

She shivered. 'It is always so cold in this dreadful house. In the great house in Briton Ferry I was always warm – there were hundreds more fireplaces than there are in this cold, dreary, awful place. Yes – my warmest gown, Sarah, if you please.'

Awful place? It seemed like a palace to me. Sarah caught my eye and pulled a face.

She went to the long chest in the corner and opened the lid, rummaging through a pile of fabric, all of it black, as far as I could see, but then, what else would a fine lady wear? Black is the most expensive dye of all, so naturally a person would wear black if she could afford to do so. Sarah drew out a heavy dress and laid it on top of the chest. When the lady had finished her breakfast, Sarah poured the hot water that I had carried upstairs into the basin, and stood by, a linen towel over her arm, waiting for the lady to wash her face and hands and dry them on the towel.

I waited awkwardly, wondering what I should do. Sarah soon told me.

'Don't dawdle like a goosegog in an apple pie, Tirion! Turn back the Mistress's bed-covers to air, and fold her nightgown and then look for –'

Spiders! I thought with a shudder.

'Those *dreadful things!*' the Mistress finished for her.

54

All very well for her. I was just as scared of them as she was, but it was my job to seek them out, when that was the last thing I wanted to do. I tried not looking very hard, but the walls of the Lady's bedchamber were cream-washed, and anything black and hairy would have stood out a mile against the pale walls. I admit, I saw one, a small one, but luckily it scuttled behind the bed before I could get to it – and before the Mistress noticed it, so I pretended not to have seen it.

When the Mistress was dressed, bum roll tied in place, her laces hauled tight and tied at the back of her bodice,[9] Sarah brushed her hair, plaited it and and tucked it under a white coif. By then I had stripped back the bedcovers and we were allowed to curtsey and leave.

Downstairs in the servants' quarters, I breathed again, and hoped that the lady would not notice any spiders. Ever.

'Here,' Catrin handed me a long stick with a bunch of goosefeathers tied to the end of it. 'This will help you reach the cobwebs and get every last one down. There is a little stool you can carry with you because

[9] Rich ladies, who had servants to help them dress, had their bodices laced at the back. Those who did it themselves wore theirs at the front!

you are not tall. I will come with you to show you about as this is your first day, but take care to remember, because tomorrow you will have to find your own way. Come on, now. The Great Hall and the Withdrawing Room have to be spick and span before the Master and Mistress come down.'

I took a deep breath and set off behind Catrin, clutching my goosefeather stick.

My Journal

Well, Mam, I slept well here at Llancaiach, although not quite as comfortable as my little cupboard bed back home. I must sleep in the attic with the other female servants, and the floor is a little hard. I had to get up before the birds were awake, and help Sarah Parry to take the Mistress's breakfast. I shall have to take it up if Sarah and Catrin are both away.

The Mistress is very grand, but you will never GUESS what she puts on her face to stop her getting Wrinkles. I shall not Write it, but I will Whisper it to you when I come Home. You will be Shocked and Amazed, I expect.

About my wonderful new Position.* Sarah Parry says that it is a very Responsible position, and I must take care to Work Hard. I promise that I shall, Mam, although some of it may prove Difficult. I am not very Homesick,** although I Confess that I do miss you a little. Please tell my Dear Stepfather that I shall never Forget his Kindness in obtaining this Position for me. One day I hope I may show my Gratitude in a Truly Appropriate manner.

*Please God, forgive me if I tell little white lies
**Even though I cried myself to sleep, I won't tell Mam that.

Chapter Six

'So,' Catrin said, inquisitively, as she led the way up the Grand Staircase to show me round the house, 'your stepfather spoke up for you to Bleddyn Cook, did he? There's kind.'

I swallowed what I would really have liked to say about my stepfather, which was very rude, and contented myself with, 'yes'.

'Your Dada died of the plague, didn't he? Oh, your poor Mam! I am a widow myself, and so I know how it must have been for her. Mind, I do not want to marry again. I would feel I was betraying my Robert if I married again, after losing him in such circumstances.'

I wished my Mam had felt the same. 'Did your Robert die of the plague, too?'

'No. My poor Robert was killed defending our home from wicked men. Deserters, they were, from the King's army, trying to steal our cattle and sheep. I blame the King. He should have made them behave better. I would not like the Master to hear me say it, mind, he would think me disloyal. But I am luckier than some. I still have my son, Geraint, to tend what animals we have left, although he is living with his Uncle Ieuan and helping on his farm, while struggling also to keep our own place alive. My girl Elen and I are lodging with my sister in Gelligaer, because it is too far to go all the way home each night.'

'When the plague took my Dada,' I said, miserably, 'we thought we had escaped, because we did not live in the town, where there was a red cross[1] painted on nearly every door. He might have escaped it,[2] too, but my Dada was a parson, and he

---

[1] If plague was in a house, a big red cross was painted on the front door to warn people to keep away. The people in the house were sealed up inside until they either got better – or didn't. At night, carts would be driven through the street with a man calling 'Bring out your dead.' Any dead people were then brought outside and driven away on the cart for burial in a common grave with hundreds of other people. In case you're feeling a bit under the weather and are worried that you may have the plague, it begins with a chill, then you get a fever and you throw up and get delirious, then there's the headaches, the blisters, the boils, the terrible pain. So don't worry. It's probably your imagination, or maybe you've just got a cold . . .

[2] Sometimes the cure was worse than the disease! There was stuff like squashed snails and moles' blood and horse wee in medicine in those days, and odd bits of dead criminals were used to cure just about everything, even toothache! Thank goodness someone discovered aspirin!

tried to look after his people. He probably caught plague from the poor families he visited.' I shuddered. 'It was horrible to see him die,' I said, remembering the terrible fever and the way Mam had nursed him without worrying that she might catch it herself.

'Aye,' Catrin sighed, 'indeed it is a terrible, terrible thing. Hannah Saer, poor child, also lost her father that way, and Sarah Parry lost her whole family – twelve years ago, it was, in the Bedwellty plague, but still she grieves. Oh, that was an awful, dreadful time. So many died that there was no time to bury the dead – they pulled up the flagstones in the church and tipped them in, all the dead people, in a heap. They say there were near two hundred of them! Shovelled like rubbish under the church, they were, poor things.'

I shivered, not liking such talk, for it reminded me of Dada, and I did not like to be reminded of how he died.

At the top of the stairs there was a large room, a fire blazing in the hearth, its walls not whitewashed like most of the house, but painted a rich, creamy yellow. A long table stood at the far end with solid, important-looking chairs behind it, and many other tables and benches were set out in the rest of the room. We didn't linger there, we went on into the room next door, the Withdrawing Room, where the family sat and took their ease. Mrs Ann Thomas, the Housekeeper, was overseeing the setting of the table for dinner,[3] and Hannah and Verity Jones were scuttling about with platters and beakers. Verity, the Under-Chambermaid, and Hannah's best friend, glanced up and winked at me in a friendly way.

'The Master and Mistress take their dinner at half-past ten, because it is winter,' Catrin whispered. 'Eleven o'clock in summer, but earlier in winter because of the dark nights.'

Mrs Ann glanced at me. 'Today the Great Hall next door is empty, Tirion, but it is used as a court once a week, and for Petty Sessions every Quarter Day. Colonel Prichard is a very important person in Glamorganshire. He is known as a good, plain-dealing, fair judge, and his opinions are greatly respected.'

'Seventy smelly common people we get in by here, Quarter Days,' Hannah sniffed.

---

[3] There would have been only two chairs at the table, when the family ate, because the children would have had to stand up to eat. Children weren't allowed to use adult furniture, so little Mary, who was only 3, would have had to stand on a box at every meal.

'And sometimes gentry when the Master entertains,' Mrs Ann said, 'and some of them are just as smelly.'[4] She smiled, and covered her mouth. 'Best not let the Master hear me say so, mind! Not Christian, to make personal remarks!'

The Withdrawing Room was panelled in new, light wood, like the great staircase, almost as pale as honey. There was a wonderful smell of woodsmoke from the blazing fire, and I wanted to go and warm my hands, which were still half-frozen from the night before. At this rate, my old problem of chilblains would soon be back, and there's real misery for you, with the itching and burning and soreness.

'Here's the House of Commons,' Catrin whispered, drawing aside a curtain to the left of the

---

[4] Everybody was smelly in those days: even the King and Queen, although they might have been slightly less unpleasant to be near than everyone else, because they could afford perfume to sprinkle on themselves to hide the pong, and lots of different clothes to wear. There weren't any dry-cleaners, you see, and although their linen underclothing was washed (and strung on tenterhooks to dry) their outer clothes were rarely washed or cleaned, only brushed, because they were made of fabric that couldn't be washed, being embroidered and ornamental. So no matter how rich you may have been, you still smelled! Oh, and you would have had fleas. And head-lice. So you would have been smelly, itchy and scratchy.

fireplace. I gazed in, and all the mystery was finally solved. There was a wooden seat with a round hole cut in it, and when I looked down, I could see a shaft dropping down towards the bottom of the house.

'It goes down the drain and into the Caiach brook a whole seventy-five yards away,' Catrin said, proudly, 'and we are the only house to have our jakes[5] indoors. Very convenient it is, for the gentry, but we servants still have to go and sit in the *tŷ-bach* over the stream to do our business, and a cold old business it is, this weather. Mind you,' she said thoughtfully, 'if this cold snap continues, young Ifor will be dangled down the privy with his candle and his little shovel and scraper to scrape the offerings away, else it will get smelly in here, and we can't have that, can we?'

I stared at her in horror. 'Ifor has to go down the privy shaft?'

Catrin chuckled. 'Oh, aye, that he does. Thirty-five feet deep, it is! He complains every step of the way, mind, and the first time Jenkin Jones, the groom –

[5] Another name for the House of Commons was 'garderobe'. There were garderobes in old castles, too – usually emptying directly into the moat – and if you look you can still see them. They were the forerunners of our wardrobes, because people kept their clothes in there to discourage the moths from eating them. Another reason why everyone ponged!

Verity's husband, you know – had to prod him with a sharp stick to make him go at all, because even the threat of a good beating didn't work.'

I never thought I'd ever feel sorry for Ifor, but having to dangle on a rope down there? Ugh!

'I can tell you, Tirion, when he comes out again he has no friends at all until he has scrubbed himself from head to toe, twice, but John Bolitho says he is a better Christian for it.'

We turned back into the main room. Catrin glanced over her shoulder suddenly, then dropped her voice to a whisper. 'Tirion, if you look up there, high on the wall, you will see the Steward's spy-hole. He has an office up there, with its own stairs, and a close-stool.[6] He can be up there and you not know it, so take care if you are in here and don't be tempted to touch anything, because he may be watching you, and you wouldn't know it. Woe betide you if you are caught snooping, or doing something you shouldn't be doing. He caught Ifor in the room, just looking, mind, for I don't believe Ifor

---

[6] Another name for a loo! A close-stool is a chair or a built-in seat with a po in it, and a lid, this time. And no flush to dispose of it, either. No. *Someone* – usually someone lowly like Ifor or even Tirion – had to carry it out and dump it, probably in the nearest stream . . . There were two close-stools in Llancaiach, as well as the four privies. Very Posh!

is wicked despite his mischief, and he was beaten for it. You, you can go anywhere in the house, but you must always remember your place.'

I glanced at the sinister little square spy-hole, and promised myself I'd be very, very careful in this room. Mind you, I wasn't sure about Ifor not being wicked!

'Why did you pull a face in the Mistress's bedroom?' I asked, remembering, 'when she said about Briton Ferry?'

'Oh, she is always on about how grand her last home was, and how much she hates Llancaiach Fawr. She is one of the Mansells of Margam, and she is afraid she has come down in the world by marrying the Colonel. Always on about Briton Ferry she is – it was larger and warmer and better furnished and all the rest of it. Oh, she doesn't know when she is well off, I can tell you!' Catrin grinned. 'Wants to try sleeping in that old attic, then she'd know all about warm and cold, wouldn't she? Well, enough gossip,' she said, prodding me, 'there is a huge cobweb up in that corner, waiting for you. Get at it, girl. I will go and help next door until you have finished brushing in here, and then I will take you upstairs.'

When she had bustled out, I stared fearfully at the

cobweb. It stretched from one corner of the panelling to the top of the fireplace. It was a big web, thick and heavy. It didn't belong to a money spider, oh no. It had to be a big one. Perhaps even a Cardinal spider.[7] With my goosefeather stick held out like a spear, I edged reluctantly closer. The web got bigger and scarier. *And I couldn't even see the spider yet!*

I reached up, and could see my whole arm trembling. I stretched out the stick towards the great, fearful, sinister spiderweb. I wanted to close my eyes, but what if the spider jumped on the stick and ran down it and *got on my hand?* If I kept my eyes open, at least I'd see it.

I jumped about a mile in the air when a voice spoke behind me.

'Who are you?'

I turned. A girl, perhaps a little older than me, stood in the doorway. I realised that this must be the Master's daughter, Jane, for she was wearing a warm blue kirtle of good cloth.

I bobbed a curtsey. 'I am Tirion Griffiths, Miss Jane.'

'Are you the spider-brusher instead of Nan? Is it

---

[7] After Cardinal Wolsey, King Henry VIII's Chancellor, who had seen one on a curtain and almost had a heart attack at the size of it!

your task to catch the spiders so that Mama won't be afraid?'

I couldn't help it. I pulled a face. 'Yes, Miss, it is, Miss.'

'Then why do you not do your work and pull down the big web in the corner? I think you are lazy. I think I shall tell Mama.'

'I shall do it at once, Miss,' I said, and curtseyed again, politely, because she was the Mistress's daughter. But I felt like pulling her hair.

Miss Jane frowned. 'Do it at once, girl,' she commanded, and left the room, leaving me alone to face the web – and its owner.

I shut my eyes. I wanted to burst into tears.

This time it was a familiar voice. 'It's a great, big, huge, horrible spider,' Ifor said. 'It has legs like tree-trunks and long fangs to bite you with. You are scared, aren't you?'

It was bad enough having to face a spider, let alone be scolded, bossed *and* laughed at while I was doing it. Without even thinking I swept the goose-feather stick across the web and pulled it away. If the spider had come running out at me I should probably have fainted on the spot. But it didn't, and I was able to step quickly away, and snootily say, 'Of course not, Ifor. And you shouldn't be in this room, should you? You aren't allowed up here, are you? You're only the spit-boy.'

'And you're –'

A large hand reached round the doorway and grabbed his ear.

'Ow!' Ifor yelped, staggering backwards, towed by his ear. 'Gerroff! That hurts!'

'As it was meant to,' Steffan Mathias, the Master's Agent said grimly. 'Be about your business, boy. And you, girl, whatever your name is, there is another web over there,' he pointed at the window, 'and half a dozen in the Great Hall, so stop chattering and lolly-gagging and get on with your work. You are not here to stand about idle. You are here to work.'

I decided I didn't like Master Mathias, the Agent, and I would avoid him if at all possible, even if he did try to pull Ifor's ear off. Meanwhile, there were the spiderwebs . . .

My Journal

I am learning more about the Other servants here at Llancaiach, Mam, and I will tell you all about them when I come Home.

Today I met Miss Jane, the Master's eldest daughter. She is twelve, older than me, and has just been Allowed to sit down to eat her dinner with the family. She eats lots of beef, and is Allowed to drink Red Wine. I have never tasted wine. Miss Mary is sweet and funny, but Miss Jane is quite solemn.*

* In fact, Miss Jane is very bossy and unkind and I do not like her. She is only a girl like me, even if she is Colonel Prichard's daughter, and she should not speak to me the way she did. But I couldn't put that in Mam's Journal, because Master Eyes and Ears would have seen it, and then I should be beaten next time I went home.

Chapter Seven

The days and weeks passed, and several times I went home to Mam bearing my other Journal – this one, mind, stayed behind, well hidden in my blankets, although (so far as I could tell, anyway) only Hannah Saer could have read it. Hannah can read and write a little. James Nicholas the serving man has begun to teach her, but she boasts about it, and the other servants don't like it, and so I am keeping quiet.

It was lovely going home and seeing Mam, but it was not so lovely seeing my stepfather and horrible Siôn. And I hated saying goodbye to Mam and beginning the long, cold journey back, some of the way on foot, because Wil-bach was too busy to take me the whole way. But with a good Welsh wool cloak, I was dry and warm and walking is what God gave us feet for, after all.

When I got back last time my nose was bright red and running because of the cold, but the rest of me was warm, for I had walked the last five miles. In the Servants' Hall at supper, Ifor sat beside me, stuffing bread and honey into his mouth, and I was just sopping my bread in the last of my *cawl*[1] when I felt him tug at my plait, where it hung down from my cap. I twitched it away crossly and glared at him, and he got up and slouched away, grinning.

Horrible boy.

I didn't know how horrible until I got up to the attic and tried to undo my plait. It was sticky, and I could hardly unbend the twined hair, because he had smeared it thickly with honey, which had dried and hardened, and my hair felt like a bunch of sticky twigs. It hurt so much, untangling it. Tears prickled in my eyes at the pain as I tried to separate the strands. I could have used the pretty ivory comb that Mam gave me for my birthday last year, but it was dark in the attic and I could not find it without lighting a candle and waking the others.

I think I hate Ifor, even though I am a good Christian girl and should not hate anybody. But then, God doesn't have an Ifor to torment Him, does he? I had to wash my hair in cold water in the morning, and then was freezing cold for hours because there was no time to sit and dry it by the fire. My cap had to be tied onto wet hair, which made me feel cold all over until it was dry.

---

[1] Broth made from vegetables (mainly) and meat.

But there is good news, too. I am not quite so afraid of spiders any more – well, not very, and then only the great big horrible black ones that scuttle so fast, or sit on their webs and *dare* me to squash them. I suppose when a person gets used to a thing, it stops being so scary. If you have to go and confront the thing that frightens you all the time, well then, if you don't die of the fright straight away, you get on with it, don't you? Mind, the funny thing is, there don't seem to be any big huge spiders any more. Perhaps I've killed them all, or frightened them off and they've moved somewhere else. Perhaps into the men's attic, to crawl all over horrible Ifor. I hope!

I know the other servants better, now. At night they tell their stories, and it helps me to understand them better. Enid Samuel is the dairymaid (the last one died of snakebite! Ugh!)[2] Enid is a cheerful person, and can be counted on to see the best side of any situation. She is very clever, too. She knows all about animals. Colonel Prichard says that what Enid does not know about horses and cows can be written

---

[2] This must have been fairly unusual even in 1645, because the only venomous snakes in Britain then, as now, were adders. But people weren't so healthy in those days, or so well-fed, and there was no anti-venin, so perhaps the poor milk-maid had an allergic reaction – for which there would have been no epi-pen injection to cure it, of course!

on the head of a pin. Hannah told me that. Enid is far too modest a person to boast.

You can always tell when Hannah Saer is about, because she smells of cloves and orange and lavender from the pomander that dangles from her belt.[3] Sometimes Verity, who gossips with her until Bleddyn Cook or Master Bolitho tells them off, teases her, but Hannah takes no notice. She is certain that it was the pomanders they carried that protected her mother and her brother's families from the plague.[4] Perhaps if my Dada had carried one – but then, he went close to the sick people, and so he smelled the disease and caught it. Perhaps he didn't even know that he smelled it. I think he was very brave.

My favourite people are Catrin Howell and Verity, because Catrin was kind to me when I came here first, and she always takes my part against Ifor. She

---

[3] A Pomander is sometimes simply an orange stuck with cloves, or perhaps if a person was richer, a ball of pierced tin to let out the scent of dried orange peel, dried flowers, herbs and other good-smelling things.

[4] You know the nursery rhyme, 'Ring-a-ring-a-roses, a pocket full of posies'? Well, that song originated during an outbreak of the plague in the Middle Ages in Britain – the 'ring-a-roses' was the rash that people got, and the 'pocket full of posies' was the pomander or the flowers they carried to sniff. And remember the last line? 'Atishoo, atishoo, aaaallll faaalllll dooooown.' Dead, actually!

smacked him for putting honey in my hair, and his ear was red for two days. She has promised to teach me to play the harp when she has time. She plays often for the Master and Mistress's entertainment, and for their guests, and I should love to be able to play as sweetly as she does – or play at all for that matter! I like Verity Jones because she is kind and funny and loves to chatter – even to me, and I know that I am not a very important person at all in the house. Or anywhere else, I suppose.

The nights are getting warmer, now, and soon I shall be sleeping out under the eaves in the cool, and the draught that whistles through the roof will be a cooling breeze instead of a finger of ice that makes me shiver with cold. Ha! Then those senior servants huddling close to the chimney will be sorry, because the fire in the kitchen burns all the time, day and night, winter and summer, so they will swelter, and I shall be cool.

Fifteen servants live here in the house, and about as many that go home at the end of the day, but still there is always so much to do. The children's nursemaids sleep up a flight of stairs from the birthing chamber, where Miss Jane and Miss Mary sleep, so that if either of them want something at night, the nursemaids will hear them call.

I ask a lot of questions, but some people don't like that. They think I should mind my own business and not pry into theirs, but there are times when I can't help it. Perhaps I am a naturally curious person. But if I don't ask, how will I ever learn anything?

When Jenkin Jones the groom, Verity's husband, came into the kitchen carrying of all things, a dead hedgehog, I was Very Curious. And when he gave it, grinning, to Sarah Parry, I was Very, Very Curious!

'What– ?' I began, but Sarah gave me a hard stare and sent me to the Mistress's chamber to look for spiders, although I had only just done it. But later I asked Hannah while I was helping her wring the linen and hang the wet laundry on tenterhooks to dry.[5]

Hannah snorted with laughter, and nudged me. 'Knew you were dying to ask!' she teased.

'Well, tell me! What does Sarah want with a dead old hedgehog?'

---

5 You may have heard the saying 'He was on tenterhooks about it!' Well, that means someone is all tense and fretful and waiting for something. The word comes from the racks – tenterhooks – that were used to spread clothes on to dry in the days before washing lines and tumble dryers. Apparently one of King Charles II's girlfriends didn't have any tenterhooks, because she used to spread her underwear on bushes in the palace garden, which greatly shocked a very important church person who happened to see them!

'It's spring, silly. And in spring the fleas go mad, especially in the Mistress's clothes, for she's plagued with them, and forever scratching, and what with her headlice, too! Honestly, I swear I saw her coif move by itself the other day while I was making the bed and she was sitting beside it, sewing. The hedgehog will get rid of the fleas.'

'It will?'

'Ever such an old recipe, my Mam used to swear by it. It was me told Sarah about it, and the Mistress is willing to try anything, the itch is making her so miserable. You roast the hedgehog over the fire, and catch the fat that drips from it. Then you coat a stick with the fat and put it near the clothes. The fleas smell the hedgehog fat, and because fleas live on hedgehogs, they jump onto the stick and – stick to it! Simple!'

I don't know if it worked, but the Mistress was still scratching even after the poor old hedgepig had been roasted, much to Bleddyn Cook's disgust, on his cooking fire. Mind, I found myself watching the Mistress's coif whenever I was near her, to see if it wriggled, which got me a clipped ear from Sarah once or twice, because I was so busy staring that I missed some cobwebs!

When the weather warmed up in the middle of

May, I was in for a shock. All the high-up servants that had huddled toasty warm next to the chimney all winter now decided they'd sleep under the eaves in the cool! So I have been turfed out of my nice cool place and forced to sleep next to the hot chimneys! It is so hot I would take off my skin and sleep in my bones if I could, so I sleep as badly in summer as I did in winter.

Ifor suffers the same way – except he suffers all day as well. It is his job to turn the spit so that the meat cooks evenly, and there has to be cooked meat[6] for dinner even in summer, except when it is Lent, when everybody eats fish instead. He has a wooden screen to hide behind, covered with straw soaked in cold water, but it doesn't help much, and he is usually bright red and blotchy and sweating whenever I see him. Good. He is a horrible boy and he deserves to suffer.

I escaped the house one night, after I had been sent upstairs to bed. That was probably very wicked of me, but it was so hot that rather than spend sleepless hours tossing in the oven-attic, I sneaked out into the cool night for a while. I wished I could

---

6 As well as beef and pork and lamb and venison, the Prichards would also have eaten heron, thrushes, sparrows, crows and seagulls, and in Lent fish, including wriggly black eels . . .

sleep out of doors under the stars. But that would have scandalised everyone. In fact, if Mrs Ann or Master Mathias had caught me I would have been in big trouble anyway, for disobeying and not going to bed.

I wandered towards the stables and spent a few moments in the moonlit yard stroking velvety noses and letting the horses blow in my ears – very peaceful creatures, horses at night. The air was sweet and cool, and the clean smell of the beasts was nicer than the hot, sweaty, stifling air in the attic. Then I heard a strange noise.

Someone was crying.

I stood in the moonlight, listening, then followed the sound. It was coming from the darkness inside the stable. I peered over the half-door. I could just see a darker heap in the shadows. I knew by the size of the heap that it was a boy – and there was only one boy in the household. *Good,* I thought, unkindly, *someone has probably beaten him. Serves him right.* But – he really was crying very, very hard.

'Ifor?' I called, softly. 'Is that you?'

'No!' he said. 'It isn't me at all. It's someone else. Go away, now Tirion, or I shall have to hit you, very hard.'

He snuffled and sobbed again, and I cannot bear

to hear anyone unhappy, no matter how much of a pest he may be. And Ifor is certainly a pest. He has done nothing but torment me since I came to Llancaiach – pretending to put spiders down my back, smearing honey in my hair, even making ghostly noises when I was going up the dark stairs to the attic. He deserves to suffer.

All the same, I pushed open the stable door – taking care to shut it behind me in case the Master's best horse ran away and I should be blamed – and crept inside. For a bit I stood over him, not knowing quite what to do, but then I remembered my Mam. I bent down.

'There, there now,' I said, patting his back, 'there there. Have a good cry.'

'I am not crying! Go away, I said! And *cau dy geg*, Tirion Griffiths, also! Because if you tell anyone that you saw me cry I will kill you dead as a doornail.'

'Don't be silly,' I said, and patted some more. 'I will shut my mouth, but I wouldn't tell on you anyway. You can't help being unhappy. I cry sometimes, because I miss my Mam.'

'But you're a girl. Girls always cry. Men don't.'

'I never saw the point of that,' I said, honestly. 'I don't think any less of you than I did before.' *I couldn't possibly have, because before that I hated him!*

79

'Won't you tell me what the matter is, though? Has Bleddyn Cook beaten you for something? Are you hurt?'

He rolled over, and sat up, sniffing. 'No. I am not hurt. What is wrong is worse than an old beating. All I want to do is to be out here, with the horses. I want to be a stable boy, and perhaps a groom, like Jenkin Jones. I'm good with horses. They understand me when I talk to them. But Master Mathias has said that I am not to be trusted, because he caught me in the Withdrawing Room last week, and Miss Jane caught me there the week before that, and told on me, and, and, and – I shall never be a groom now.'

Horrible Miss Jane, telling tales! Catrin thought she was an angel, but angels didn't tell tales on people to get them in trouble the way Miss Jane did. I sat back on my heels and stared at him. 'What? Ifor ap Iestyn, I can't believe you were daft enough to go back in that room after you had already been caught! What on earth for?'

'Well, I wasn't looking to steal anything! I wasn't, no matter what Master Mathias thinks. I'm not a thief. I was only – oh, never mind.'

'Tell me!' I said, sternly. I can do a very good stern voice, because I learned it from my Mam.

'Can't you guess, you stupid girl, you? I have been

80

sneaking up there where I am not allowed so I could catch all the big spiders for you, so you wouldn't have to. I know what it is like to be afraid of something. I don't like snakes and I hate wasps.'

I stared at him. So that was why there had been so few spiders lately! 'But you are always tormenting and teasing me!' I said, stupidly.

'I only did that to make you feel at home,' he wailed. 'Oh, go away. I shall never be a groom now, or even a stable boy, and it is all your fault.'

'But I didn't ask you to –'

'Oh!' he said passionately, 'O, *cau dy geg a cer o 'ma!*

So I did what he ordered. I shut my mouth and went away.

But I thought and thought about Ifor the spit boy from then on. I stopped thinking of him as nothing but a stupid nuisance, and a tease, like all boys, and began to see that perhaps he was kind, even though I still couldn't see how honey in my hair would make me feel at home. But he had been kind behind my back, which is worth more, my Dada used to say. He had hidden his light under a bushel.[7] So. How could I do a kindness for him in return?

---

[7] Hiding your light under a bushel means that you do someone a good turn or a kindness – and you don't tell anyone about it! Doing good by stealth is another way of putting it.

If I were really brave, I would have gone to see Master Mathias and explained to him what Ifor had been doing in the Withdrawing Room when he should not have been there.

But although I wasn't nearly so afraid of spiders any more, I was certainly afraid of Master Mathias, and I didn't have the courage even to look at him, let alone tell him he was wrong about Ifor! Oh, why can't I be brave?

When I saw Miss Jane in the passageway later, I scowled at her. I hate a tale-teller. I wish I could tell tales on her, because she is not perfect. I don't think she noticed my black looks, however. She doesn't notice a person like me, unless she is catching me out doing something wrong. Then she notices quick enough!

My Journal

The Weather is very hot here, Mam, and in our attic where we all Sleep there sometimes does not appear to be enough Air to go round. I sometimes Wake up with a Headache, because of the heat, but kind Catrin makes me a cup of Nettle tea just like you used to Do, which makes me feel Better.

Do you remember, Mam, I for the spit-boy that I wrote that I would Pray for, to help him be a Better boy? Well, I think perhaps my Prayers are working, because he is a Kinder boy than I Thought. I shall Pray twice as hard as before to make him Better Quicker. He is not a Happy Boy, and like me, he does not have a Father. His father is dead, like my Dada.

PS Although of course I do not forget Dear Stepfather. I shall Remember him, I promise, and all he has done for me.

Chapter Eight

Quite soon, however, Ifor got over his miseries and went on being the teasing, difficult boy he usually was, so I stopped feeling sorry for him quite quickly. I got under my blanket late one night, in the dark, and got out again very fast, with a scream so loud it woke everyone in both attics.

My feet had landed on something furry and stiff and horrid, and when Hannah Saer fetched a candle, we discovered that someone – and no prizes for guessing who – had put a dead mouse in my bed! He was beaten for that trick, because my screams woke all the men as well as everyone in the women's attic. They all wanted to beat Ifor, but Bleddyn Cook was given the honour.

Ifor's latest prank was to sneak upstairs and lurk outside the Withdrawing Room where I was spider-brushing, quietly close the door behind me and wait. He'd hold it shut so that when I tried to get out, I thought it was stuck! And then, when I was tugging and pulling and rattling and beginning to panic and shout for help, he would let go, and the door would fly open and I would fall backwards, once right onto my bum in a heap. At first I thought the wooden door was sticking, so I told Siencyn ap Gwilym that the door needed fixing. He tried the door and opened and shut it, and it didn't stick at all. So then I was scolded for wasting his time.

I couldn't understand it. Why did it only stick when I was in the room? Perhaps the room was haunted, and the ghost was haunting me, personally![1]

And then, coming red-faced, flustered and a little afraid out of the Withdrawing Room early one morning I saw the 'ghost', disappearing down the stairs. Ifor again!

I could forgive him more easily now, though, because he had been catching the big spiders for me. That was a kindness, and I think his tricks are because he doesn't want me to think him soft! I shall never understand boys. They are very strange.

---

[1] Llancaiach Fawr, like any other old house worth its salt, is said to be haunted by two ghosts, a man in a cloak and a tall hat in the gardens and on the road outside, and a lady in a long white dress. Oh, and ghostly footsteps in the Great Hall . . . Tirion, being a good Baptist girl, would not have believed in them. Or then again, she might have, because there's something about a rumour of a ghost that makes most people wonder . . .

We rubbed along from day to day, me with my chores, Ifor with his, which included scrambling into the pigeon-loft in Colonel Prichard's study. He had to catch the birds so they could be sent with messages tied to their legs – perhaps to the King himself, or Prince Charles, or even the brave and handsome Prince Rupert of the Rhine.[2]

And then, in the middle of long (and sometimes boring) days, two exciting things happened: one good, the other bad, so bad that it set the whole house in an uproar and made everyone unhappy and out of sorts. It was July, and the weather was so hot that everyone was in a wicked temper with it, and there was no way of being cool in the Servants' Hall because of the great

[2] Prince Rupert was King Charles I's nephew. He was 25 in 1645. He was a sort of Civil War pin-up-boy, being very brave and handsome, riding a big white horse and all that stuff. Everywhere he went he was accompanied by Boy, his white poodle. It was said that Boy was either ghostly or magical, depending on who was telling the story. Some people said that the dog was a devil in disguise, and a spy at Rupert's command . . . Mind, I expect it still had fleas! It was killed by a Roundhead at the Battle of Marston Moor because somebody forgot to tie it up. Rupert is also supposed to have stopped for an ice-cream on the way to the Battle of Naseby (he lost that one) but since ice-cream was a very new invention, that may not be true, but is a Good Story. In later life he became a Pirate, and was also the director of the Canadian Hudson's Bay fur-trading Company. He was nicknamed 'The Mad Cavalier'.

fire in the kitchen next door that must be kept constantly burning. Bleddyn Cook was a monster of fury from morning until night because of the heat and having to cook so close to it, for the Master still had to have his dinner even when each step brought sweat trickling beneath our heavy clothes. Poor Ifor was clouted up hill and down dale because he was the nearest and the youngest, and as Master Bleddyn put it, 'If you haven't done anything wrong this time, then the beating will do for next time.' Only by next time, him being old and forgetful, Bleddyn usually gave him another, so then he had two, and one for nothing!

Upstairs, the window in the Colonel's study – the only one in the house that could be opened – had been flung open to catch the slightest breeze, because the house was stifling. If the wind was in the right (or perhaps the wrong) direction, the stink of the Caiach Brook drifted in through the open doors despite the lavender and the thyme and the lemon balm in the Knot Garden, and made everybody feel sick. There were flies everywhere, despite the blue jugs of fragrant herbs and scented flowers that stood everywhere.[3] Of

---

[3] It was believed that flies disliked strong scents and also the colour blue. So having fragrant flowers everywhere in blue jugs would keep flies out of the house. Perhaps it never occurred to people that the garden was FULL of fragrant flowers – and flies . . .

course, our jakes hung over the stream summer and winter, and the indoor jakes were sluiced into it from the house, so no wonder it smelled when the weather got hot. I felt sorry for the villagers downstream, who had the filthy, stinking water flowing past their houses, and sometimes into them, if it rained very hard and the brook flooded. They took their water from it to wash and perhaps even to drink, too, and the village children splashed in it to get cool, and the smell and the flies must have been horrible when it was so hot.

But that happens every year, I expect, and the exciting things didn't. The first thing that happened was that the Master lost one of his silver buttons, the ones that decorate his Sunday-best coat.[4] He left twelve shiny buttons on his desk in his study, but when he came back, there were only eleven. At first he thought perhaps he had knocked one to the floor without noticing, and it had rolled out of sight, but despite the Master and John Bolitho and Steffan Mathias looking all over the study, it was not found. Hannah Saer and I were sent to search the paths outside under the trees and in the garden, in case he

---

[4] You may think it is weird not having his buttons sewn on – but because they were silver ones, and special, Colonel Prichard would have swapped them from coat to coat!

had lost it while walking after his Sunday dinner, but although we searched until it was almost too dark to see, we didn't find it. And then – oh, it was terrible, awful – a *second* button disappeared from the table where the others had been left while we searched, and the Master declared, with a face like thunder and a voice to match, that there must be a thief in the house! And when the thief was found, he or she would be turned off, or worse.[5]

We servants were set to searching the whole house high and low, inside presses, inside cupboards, under the sea-grass matting on the floors, under the furniture, inside the beds, on top of cupboards, inside chests, in the little cupboards in the panelled walls where the wine is kept. We didn't find the missing buttons.

Worse still, Ifor the spit-boy was suspected of having stolen them, because he is the boy who goes into the pigeon loft in the Master's study to fetch the birds for the Master's messages. His bedding in the

---

[5] Being 'turned off' meant you were given the sack without a reference, which means you couldn't get another job. And it could have been much, much worse – sometimes people were hanged for stealing, or branded with hot irons and other unpleasant things – although of course it did make for a jolly good day out for the local people when the sentence was carried out.

men's attic was searched (as was all our bedding, but Ifor's most carefully of all) but I am glad to say that nothing was found anywhere. It would be horrid to think that one of the other servants was a thief.

The constable was called from Bedlinog, and he threatened Ifor with all kinds of terrible punishments, but Ifor swore he was honest, and would not be shaken. But all the same, the buttons were still lost, and Steffan Mathias was heard to mutter that a certain boy who had been caught lurking in rooms where he had no right or permission to be, must naturally be a thief, although he, Steffan Mathias could not prove it. Me, I don't believe that Ifor is a thief, and neither does Catrin or Hannah or Verity. We know that he is mischievous, but we would swear that he is honest as the day is long.

There was as much evidence against any of us as there was against Ifor, and yet he was the only one who suffered, just because he had been caught in the Withdrawing Room and had to go in the Master's study because of the pigeons.

I felt guilty, because if Ifor had not been catching spiders for me, he would not have been there in the first place, would he? I offered to tell Master Mathias, but Ifor swore horribly at me, and said that if I opened my mouth he would strangle me and bury me in the herb garden, because he did not want the other servants ever to know that he had been soft as a stupid girl in helping me, and he wished he hadn't bothered, so there.

The second thing – the nice thing – we heard about while Hannah and I were making the Master's bed. I was bending down, pushing John Bolitho's truckle bed in under the Master's, all made up ready for the night, and Hannah was smoothing the top cover of the short little bed. It is not short and little because the Master is a very small man,[6] or because he can't afford a bigger one. Hannah says that some grand people believe that if they sleep sitting up, if the Angel of Death happens to be passing, he will think the person is wide awake and sitting up and will pass them by. If they are lying down, he will take them. Mind you, John Bolitho has to sleep lying down, and so do I, and my Mam and all the other servants, and we are all still here! Not that the Master is silly and superstitious, mind. No, his physician has advised him to sleep that way, for his health's sake. He sleeps sitting up so that the evil

---

[6] In fact, Colonel Prichard was five feet ten inches tall – about 1.8 metres. Quite tall for people in those days, who didn't have the benefits that we have today – like milk and vitamins and friendly-bacteria-yoghurt-drinks.

humours[7] of the night will drain away. So it would be a waste to have a long bed, wouldn't it?

But that is by-the-by: I was telling you about the Exciting Thing. There we were, making the beds, when Sarah Parry rushed in with the news she had overheard while tidying the Mistress's bedchamber. The Master has had a letter, and it has put him AND the whole household in a bate, especially the Mistress, Steffan Mathias and Bleddyn ap Thomas, Cook.

His Majesty King Charles I is coming to dinner *here*.[8] Yes, here, to Llancaiach! Perhaps I shall see the King! Me, Tirion Griffiths! But then, perhaps we common servants may not be allowed. Oh, I hope we shall be! It is just over a week, now! He will be here on August 5th. And oh, I hope, I hope that I shall be allowed to see him.

---

[7] 'Evil humours' doesn't mean bad temper. In those days, people didn't know about modern medicine and they thought that everything that went wrong with a person was down to 'evil humours' – the four bodily fluids (blood, phlegm, yellow bile and black bile – don't ask!). So if you lay down to sleep, the evil humours would sort of clog you up. If you sat up – they drained away. Simple, really!

[8] You may wonder what the King was doing in Wales in the first place. Well, after he was defeated at the Battle of Naseby he retreated to Raglan Castle in Monmouthshire, home of the Earl of Worcestershire. Raglan Castle had a jolly good bowling green there (it still has, today) and the King enjoyed a game or two during his stay.

It was too hot to sleep anyway, that night, tucked as I was against the roasting hot chimney in the stifling attic, but I was too excited even to try. My mind kept saying, *the King, the King, the King is coming! I'm going to see the King!*

Poor Bleddyn ap Thomas was most bothered, I suppose, because he had to prepare food to feed the most important person in the whole world, after God, whom I suppose does not eat. Oh. I hope that isn't blasphemy. (If it is, I am very sorry, God.[9])

So Bleddyn Cook wandered about his kitchen scratching his head and muttering about Gammon Pies, and Dishes of Carrots, and Pike, and Chicken, and a Haunch of Beef and a Whole Lamb and Half a Pig, and perhaps a Swan or a Peacock might be got.[10] Poor Ifor began to worry that his whole life might be

---

9 King James I of England, and his son King Charles I, believed that Kings were made Kings directly by God. Whatever the King said or did had to be treated as if God Himself were saying or doing it. Charles I was Very Good at being a Divine King when it came to raising taxes, and getting money out of people, and Parliament got fed up with this. It was one of the causes of the Civil War.

10 How would you like this for your Sunday dinner? Fruit tarts, soused (pickled in vinegar or brine) gammon, a kid with a pudding in its stomach, partridges, crystallised flowers (made by the Mistress) pickled oysters, buttered crabs, custard, brawn and peacock. And that was only one course! No wonder dinner started at around ten in the morning!

spent desperate with heat, crouched beside a blazing fire turning a spit, and occasionally leaping up to dip the long ladle into the dripping fat in the pan beneath to baste the roasting food.

The gardeners were set to trimming the lawn with their shears and tidying up the Knot Garden. The grooms and stable boy were set to scrubbing the stables and grooming the horses. The housemaids were put to cleaning the entire house, not only the Great Hall and the jakes, but the Withdrawing Room and the chambers and the stables and every little corner of the house that the King might possibly wish to glance at, or even accidentally notice in passing by.

I was so excited I could hardly breathe as August 5th drew closer, but the people around me got crosser and crosser. I quickly learned to keep out of everyone's way, and just do my job as well as I could. I swear that there was not one spider anywhere in the whole house, and I was dealing with all sizes now, because Ifor couldn't help any more. It was hard for me, but I discovered that if I hit even the biggest spider hard enough with my feathery stick, it was at least stunned, and I could squash it quickly before it had a chance to scuttle towards me! I wasn't as afraid of them as I once was, but that didn't mean I *liked* them!

And then, at last, it was The Day.

My Journal

It is very Busy here at Llancaiach as we wait to Welcome The King. Colonel Prichard is fussing quite a lot, and is a little Distracted. Sometimes his Wife has to speak to him Several times before he hears.

I suppose it is a Great Responsibility to welcome one's Sovereign to one's House – just Imagine, Mam, if the King came to Our house! How you would be polishing and cleaning and borrowing Good Dishes from the Neighbours! But He is not likely to visit our house, and perhaps that is fortunate.*

The gardeners have been on their hands and knees trimming the Lawn for days and days to make it neat – Imagine, Mam, being so Rich as to have a Lawn! And Miss Jane and Miss Mary are allowed to Walk on it!

* Because who would want to visit a house with my horrible Stepfather in it, and his horrible son? I admit, if it were not for my Mam being there, I should not go home at all. But to see her, I must also see Them.

Perhaps I could do some great service to the King while he is here. Perhaps I could jump on an assassin and save the King's life, or stop him drinking poisoned wine, or something like that, then the King would be so grateful that he would offer me my Heart's Desire. But would it shock the King if I said that my Heart's Desire is not for riches, but to have my horrid Stepfather shut up in prison, or better, have his head chopped off? And his horrible son's while we are at it!

Unless the King could make sure that I have a better job than Spider-brusher . . . That would be a Heart's Desire worth having!

Chapter Nine

We were woken earlier then usual on The Day. There wasn't even a lemony gleam of dawn in the east, and the birds were still asleep, but already there was the threat of heat in the very air we breathed.

We fumbled to get dressed by candlelight, me shivering with excitement, and once downstairs we were made to do again what we had been doing every single day – cleaning. Even though the house was spotless – my Mam would say you could eat off the floor! – it must be done again, so that not a speck of dust or a single cobweb disgraced the Master and Mistress's household. I felt quite important, just brushing down the spidery traces clinging in the corner of the room, because I was helping Llancaiach get ready for our King.

Before dawn Bleddyn ap Thomas was scurrying about, brandishing his ladle and his great spoon, tasting and stirring, flinging a handful of salt into a pot, grinding pepper, adding rich, expensive spices or sugar or cinnamon to a custard. The bread ovens were full, one of the Master's best lambs was spitted over the roaring fire, fat splashing and spitting as Ifor sat sweating behind his screen turning the handle of the spit. I stuck my head into the kitchen to marvel at the wonderful puddings that Bleddyn had created, and the number of pies and custards and creams and savouries that he had made – and all for one man! Then I wished I hadn't, because Bleddyn Cook spotted me and set me to scrubbing dirty pots and pans.

I scrubbed and scrubbed, elbow deep in cold, greasy water, and all the time the King was getting closer. My clean pinafore was in the attic, and my Sunday shoes, and here I was scrubbing pots! I felt like running away from the trough of filthy water. Lookouts had been posted along the road to the village, and at last one came scurrying back to say that His Majesty would arrive within the hour.

And then Master Mathias came into the kitchen, all in his Sunday best.

'You, boy,' he said, looking down at sweating Ifor, turning his spit, 'you will stay in the kitchen. And you, girl, whatever your name is, you are far too untidy and filthy to be seen. You will both stay out of sight.'

The other servants were in the Servants' Hall, tucking stray wisps of hair under spotless white caps, straightening aprons, brushing tunics and combing beards. I glanced at Ifor, still turning, turning, and the anguished expression on his red, sweaty face. We two, of everyone in the household, would miss this most important day of our lives because Ifor was suspected of being a thief and I was too dirty and lowly and unworthy to be allowed even to look at the King. Ifor's father had died fighting for him, and my Dada had prayed for him every Sunday in his Chapel, but we weren't even to be allowed to look at him. I thought I might die of misery, and I hated Master Mathias, even though it is wrong to hate anyone (although I will make an exception for my stepfather).

Bleddyn Cook would not be outside the great door of the house to bow as His Majesty arrived, either, but he would certainly be Sent For when the King had finished his Dinner. Bleddyn Cook did not mind staying in the kitchen while everyone else lined up outside in two rows flanking the door, but then he saw our miserable faces, and his harassed, red, sweating, bearded face softened.

'If nobody sees you,' he whispered, when the kitchen was empty except for us, 'if you can find a place to hide where no one can see you, not the Master, not John Bolitho or Steffan Mathias, or even

Mrs Ann, then you can go and look. Only until His Majesty is inside, mind. Then back here, both of you, or I will have your hides nailed to my kitchen wall. But if anyone sees you, I shall be in trouble too, so take care you are not found out. Go on. Go quick, before the others get outside!'

We didn't need telling twice. We hurtled out of the kitchen and down the hallway, scuttling from door to door until at last we were outside and haring down the path edging the Knot Garden.

Once outside the garden wall, Ifor panted, 'Follow me! I know a place!'

We bent low to follow the line of the wall back towards the front door, keeping well down so no one could see us. To the left of the house almost beside the front door, a tree in full summer leaf grew close to the wall.

'There!' Ifor said, 'we can hide in the branches!'

Ifor could scramble up trees like a squirrel, but because of my long skirt, I was doomed to stay at ground level. Besides, I like heights as much as I like spiders, which is not at all.

'I can't get up there!' I wailed. 'It's too high! I'm going to have to go back inside. Oh, I'm never going to see the King now!'

'Don't be such a goose,' Ifor said, scowling. 'I

thought you were brave, Tirion. Tuck up your skirt and climb. I'll go first. Go on,' he urged. 'I'll help you. I promise I won't look while your legs are showing, and you can put your kirtle down again once you are safe up the tree. Come on. You aren't afraid, are you?'

'Safe' and 'up the tree' didn't go together in my mind, but it was my choice, wasn't it? Either I climbed the tree and risked breaking my neck, or I didn't see the King. If I didn't see him I should regret it for the rest of my life. When His Majesty defeats horrible old Oliver Cromwell, he will go back to London to his Palace and I shall never have the chance again, for London is as far away as the moon. A thousand times further away even than Cardiff, and I have only been there once in my whole life.

Then, suddenly, quietly at first and far away in the distance, I heard cheering. It got louder and louder, and people were yelling 'God Save the King!' and 'God preserve Your Majesty!' and 'God Bless your Majesty!' and 'Down with Cromwell!'. If I didn't climb that tree, I should never see the King and would never forgive myself, ever, for being such a stupid coward.

Ifor had already scrambled up and was perched in the branches like an awkward, featherless bird.

'Don't look!' I hissed, and he obediently shut his eyes while I hauled my thick, full skirts between my knees and tucked the ends into my waistband, showing my over-the-knee, gartered stockings. I kicked off my old shoes and peeled off my stockings and hid them in a bush before beginning the climb. It was surprisingly easy: knobbly bits of trunk stuck out for my bare feet to grip, and with Ifor, eyes shut, stretching out his hand to pull me up the last little bit, I was quickly perched beside him. I untucked my skirt with difficulty, because I was clinging like grim death to the tree-trunk with my free arm, but at last I was decent again. Scared, but decent.

'You can open your eyes again now,' I said, and Ifor did. He was grinning. 'What?' I said, suspiciously.

'Your knees are ever so knobbly,' he said. 'Ow!'

'Serves you right for looking,' I muttered. 'You promised you wouldn't. People who break promises go to Hell.'

'You didn't have to clout me! I didn't really look. I was only teasing.'

I looked around me. The leaves rustled, and it was cooler in the tree. I glanced up at the clear blue of the sky patching the branches, and saw that we were sharing our hiding place with a magpie in a nest. It cack-crackled at us, cocked its head, glared down at us with its shiny black, angry eyes, and flapped away, scolding, cross at being turfed out of its tree by humans.

The cheering grew louder and louder, and below us the servants lined up excitedly in two rows beside the front door, men on one side, women on the other, all clean and brushed and tidier than I had ever seen them. The Mistress was standing between them, facing the gates, Jane and Mary beside her, and Colonel Prichard was riding proudly on his great roan gelding out of the great gates to meet the King.

'That's Math Mawr the Master is riding,' Ifor whispered, 'like the magician. I know all the horses in the Master's stables.'

'Hush!' I whispered back. 'Someone will hear us!'

And then His Majesty arrived!

The cheering was deafening, and below me I could see Miss Mary bouncing up and down with excitement, flapping her hands, until a stern look from the Mistress subdued her. Miss Jane had her nose in the air and was standing perfectly still with her hands clasped before her. She had on a beautiful blue dress. I shall never have a dress as fine as that one if I live to be a hundred. Miss Jane doesn't deserve it.

Colonel Prichard dismounted and bowed low, sweeping his hat from his head. The King nodded to him, and the Colonel remounted and rode beside the King towards the front door, making polite conversation. I wondered what he was saying. After all, what can you say to a King who is the next best person to God? I'm sure I couldn't think of a thing.

Just before they reached the lines of servants, His Majesty and the Master dismounted, and the grooms, smart in dark breeches and white shirts, led their horses away to the stables.

The Mistress curtseyed, and Miss Mary gave a sweet wobbly one, a look of concentration on her pink little face. Miss Jane, however, swooped down, showing off – and caught her heel in the hem of her dress and almost toppled over. The King didn't seem to notice, but I did, though, and grinned. Serve her right for telling tales on Ifor!

And then the King was right below me, facing our tree, straightening his dark coat, tugging at his lace collar, and I could see his face as close and clear as I saw Hannah Saer's on the pallet next to mine every morning!

My first feeling – which was very disrespectful and disgraceful, and might even have got my head chopped off if anyone had known – was disappointment. Whenever I thought of the King – and I didn't do that very much, except when news of battles came to the house, and things like that – I thought of someone tall and strong and handsome and amazing and – oh, I don't know – *majestic*, I suppose!

For sure, he was richly enough dressed, but in a plain dark coat and lace collar, and an ordinary hat. He wasn't wearing jewels, satins and silks the way a King should, to my mind. He stood very straight, but the hair beneath his tall hat was light, mousy brown, and his beard and moustache were wispy and fine. There was nothing, well, *extraordinary* about him at all, even though he was someone who had been made King by God!

He was handsome enough, I suppose, in an *old* sort of way, but he was *so very, very small!* If he'd been standing next to me, he would not have been much taller! Colonel Prichard towered over him by about seven inches. Does that not seem wrong, somehow? Since God had made him our King, He might have troubled to make him a great big man, too, so that he would *look* like a King!

I thought that I was keeping as still as a mouse, that no one could possibly see me hidden in the thickness of green leaves. I *thought* that I was completely invisible.

But as I looked down on my rather disappointing Sovereign, his eyes suddenly flicked upwards. And met mine.

I froze, like a rabbit when a stoat looks it in the eye. I waited for him to scream, 'Assassin! Help! Murder! Send her to the Tower! Chop off her head!' Then I should be arrested and dragged away in chains, and never go home to Mam again. I thought I might be sick with fright, because I had disobeyed Master Mathias and at the very least I would be turned off and have to go home in disgrace to my Mam and Stepfather, who would never let me forget it. I felt dizzy, and clung to my branch so that I wouldn't fall out of the tree and crash at his feet.

His eyes met mine for only an instant. They crinkled slightly at the corners, in surprise, and then they shifted away again, as if a girl hiding in a tree was quite usual. I waited, terrified, for him to tell the Master.

I didn't think he had seen Ifor, though, crouched beside me on the branch. So Ifor was safe, unless of course I was taken to the Tower and tortured on the rack and made to tell. *Even if they torture me,* I vowed silently, *I shall never betray Ifor, who is in enough trouble as it is.*

My Journal

His Majesty King Charles came to Llancaiach, Mam! He did, he did!

There! What do you think of that? All the servants* were Allowed to line up each side of the Door to Greet him when he arrived, and curtseyed and bowed as he passed between them into the House. He stayed to eat dinner with the Master and Mistress, and my Stepfather's friend Bleddyn ap Thomas cooked a wonderful Meal for him to Enjoy, and he did Enjoy it, because Bleddyn Cook was Sent For and the King told him so!.

After Dinner His Majesty and his friends rode off to Brecon, where he was to take Supper.

It was very exciting and I will tell you more about the visit when I see you.

* Except Ifor the spit-boy and me. We weren't allowed, but we saw him anyway. You don't want to know how, Mam, it would only upset you. And besides, if Master Eyes and Ears got to hear about it, I'd be eating off the mantle-piece for a month.

Which reminds me. I still haven't found a way to repay him, have I?

Chapter Ten

You will be pleased to learn that I was not dragged off to the Tower of London and tortured with hot irons and pincers and stretched on the rack until I was three yards tall.

The King, the Master and the Mistress walked past the ranked servants, nodding and smiling and then they disappeared inside the house. When they had gone, the servants, smiling and excited, scurried in after them and rushed to go about their duties and help serve dinner. As soon as it was safe, Ifor and I clambered down from our tree and fled back to the kitchens. In my excitement I forgot my shoes and stockings, and had to go back for them, but no one saw me, I'm glad to say. Soon, seeing the King was only a wonderful memory – even if he is small. Once again I was armpit-deep in cold, greasy water, and Ifor was turning and turning and turning the spit, sweat dripping from his face. But occasionally, we glanced at each other from the corners of our eyes – and grinned.

The King did not stay long: when he had eaten his dinner – and a very fine dinner it was – Bleddyn ap

Thomas the Cook was summoned to the Great Hall where the King thanked him and gave him a gold piece!

Bleddyn, of course, has no need for gold, because he is very rich already. As well as earning *ten whole pounds* a year, he already owns a cottage in Penarth, and 32 acres of land and four cows *and* some chickens and ducks that his father left him when he died. Mind, according to Sarah Parry, who knows everything, his father also left him his mother, who is a dreadful old woman with a bad temper.

Bleddyn swears he will never spend the King's gold coin, but intends to have a fine box made for it. He will keep it to show to his children when he has some, which will probably be a long time in the future because he does not have a wife yet. I think Enid Samuel would be willing if he should ask her, but his mother does not want him to wed, so Enid must wait.

Even after the King had gone, the excitement remained in the house like a special scent in the air. The Master, once he had ridden down the Brecon road with the King and said fare thee well to his Royal Visitor, called us all together and thanked us. That made all of us beam with pride, I can tell you. Even though all I did was chase spiders and wash greasy pots, it must have helped a bit, mustn't it? Without me, the King might have been so frightened by a spider that he might have had a fit and died.

In the Servants' Hall we servants chattered about the visit until bedtime, and even after that I lay awake in the hot attic listening to whispers all around me. Just before I fell asleep, I decided that the King must be a good and noble person even if he was small and rather wispy and not big and handsome and strong.

You see, when I was summoned to the Withdrawing Room after supper that evening to brush away a spider lurking in the corner, the Master and Mistress were talking. I *know* that I should not have listened. It is not a servant's place to eavesdrop on her betters, I *know* that. But I couldn't help hearing, could I? I'm not deaf. I tell you, I almost fell off my little stool when I heard.

The Master was leaning back in his chair with a glass of wine in his hand. The Master took a sip of wine, and said to the Mistress, 'My dear, I confess that there is one thing that puzzles me yet about His Majesty's visit.'

The Mistress, exhausted even though she hadn't chased any spiders or washed a single pot, raised an eyebrow. 'What is that, dearest?'

'As we rode towards Brecon, His Majesty turned to me and – well, he said the strangest thing! I have thought and thought, and still I cannot make out what he may have meant by it. I think that he was not displeased, for he was smiling – but at what I cannot imagine!'

The Mistress was concerned. 'What did he say, husband?'

'He said, my dear, "Prichard, I vow your trees bear exceeding strange fruit." And then he smiled.'

The Mistress looked puzzled.

'What *can* he have meant, do you think?' the Master asked. 'Was it was some cipher? Some code? *Should* I have known?'

'I have no idea, beloved,' the Mistress replied, and yawned.

But I had!

The spider squashed and scraped up, I was able to escape. I sat on the stairs and stuffed my apron into my mouth so that they would not hear me laugh.

But that was not the only thing that was keeping me awake, that night after the visit.

No. There was something else. Something peculiar, dancing around in the back of my mind, annoying as a buzzing fly – and there were plenty of those in our attic in the heat, I can tell you. I was fair bitten to bumps. What was bothering me? Why couldn't I remember? It was something to do with the tree . . .

In the end I just closed my eyes and tried to think of everything that had happened.

Then I remembered. I smiled a great, big smile in the hot darkness. *I wonder*, I thought drowsily as I fell asleep. *I wonder . . .*

Instead of the clear blue sky of the day of the King's visit, the following day was dull and heavy, overcast with black clouds.

Catrin mopped her face with her apron. 'There will be a thunderstorm before long, you mark my words,' she muttered. 'That will clear the air, although I am afraid of lightning. At home I hide in the wall-bed, but here I must put up with it.'

She shivered as an ominous rumble sounded in the distance. The air was like a heavy, wet blanket. Because we had all worked so hard for the Visit, we all were on light duties that day, and it would be a cold dinner because Master Bleddyn had been given the day off. So, once the Master and Mistress had finished their cold meat and left-over custard, I slipped away.

The door was standing wide open to catch any passing breeze. Out I went and down the path beside the Knot Garden like a hunted hare, then alongside the wall on the other side until I came to our tree. I looked up. I didn't want to climb it today any more than I had yesterday – but I should have to if I were to find out the truth.

So I took off my shoes and stockings again, took a deep breath, and began to climb. It was harder today, with no Ifor to help me up. Then, as I climbed, the storm broke. Rain came down as if I was climbing a waterfall, not a tree. Thunder crashed like war-cannons, and lightning flared blue-white all round me. My Dada used to say, 'Tirion, if there is a thunderstorm, you must *never* take shelter under a tree, for the tree will attract the lightning and if you are not killed by a lightning bolt, the tree may fall upon you and crush you!' And here I was climbing up one. *O, Iesu Mawr*, I prayed, *don't let me be struck by lightning just now, please!*

At last I reached where we'd perched, yesterday. I climbed even higher. The magpie's nest was a good yard[1] further up than the place we had been sitting, and the branches were thinner and more dangerous. The magpie, driven back to its nest by the storm,

---

[1] I know you don't do yards – but Tirion didn't do metres! They hadn't been invented yet. But if it helps, a yard is worth 914 millimetres

glared at me with its beady black eyes and chattered a warning. I scowled back, and shooed it away. The branch swayed alarmingly, a furious squirrel shot out of its dray even further up and I almost fell off my branch in fright.

But I kept on, and I was rewarded, because when I finally reached the magpie's nest and shooed the irritated creature away, there, hidden in the nest, were two shiny, silver buttons . . . And a silver sewing needle that the Mistress had lost while sewing in the garden one day, and a piece of shiny silk thread from her work-basket, and a silver thimble that Elisabeth Proude was certain she had lost on a visit to her Nain, and a couple of shiny sequins perhaps from some rich lady visitor's dress. I took my cap off and carefully wrapped it all up inside, tucked the cap into the waistband of my skirt, and started down again.

A particularly loud clap of thunder, followed by a lightning flash immediately overhead startled me so much that I fell the last yard down the tree, landing in an undignified and painful manner hard on my bum. But I didn't care. I had the proof that Ifor, my friend Ifor, was not a thief.

I found my shoes, but it was raining too hard to put them on. I ran for the front door, forgetting my skirts tucked up to my thighs, forgetting everything in my excitement and my hurry to be inside in the dry.

And there my good fortune ran out, for I was caught by Mrs Ann the Housekeeper, who was coming down the Great Staircase as I shot through the door. It was a great shame that the house has only one door.[2] If there had been a back door, perhaps I could have slipped in without getting caught. But I was caught, and Mrs Ann was scandalised.

'Tirion Griffiths!' she hissed. *'What* are you doing, with your legs showing! Suppose one of the men – or even the Master, Heaven help us! – had seen you? Cover yourself at once! I am shocked, shocked to my boot-soles, and you will hear more of this, my girl. Go and dry yourself at once. What were you doing out of doors in such weather?'

---

[2] You may think it is weird that a big, posh house like Llancaiach could apparently only afford one door, and had only one window in the whole house that opened. There was a good reason for this, however: it was a bit like a castle, it had to be able to be defended against attack. So the fewer doors there were to defend, and the fewer windows that opened, the better. The Withdrawing Room (or parlour) was in the safe part of the house, which could be sealed off if there was an attack – and of course, because of the House of Commons, the family could also go to the loo!

'But –!' I began, but she held up her hand to stop me.

'But me no buts, girl. Go and change at once. I shall speak to you after supper.'

So despite my excitement, I had that hanging over me all day. I looked for John Bolitho, and would have told Bleddyn Cook about the magpie, but both were away. Master Mathias was there, but I am afraid of him, and so it fell to Mrs Ann to hear my news. Which was as it should be, I suppose, because I may not speak to the senior servants without her permission anyway.

So after supper, me in my Sunday best because I had no other clothes to wear except my wet ones, was sent for by the Housekeeper to be Spoken To.

'Well?' she asked, sternly. 'What have you to say for yourself? Why were you outside, with your legs all naked, in the pouring rain? I thought you were a good girl, but I am beginning to wonder. Answer me, girl. What have you to say, Tirion Griffiths, before I send you home in disgrace?'

'If you please, Mrs Ann, I know it was wrong, but it was for a good reason. When His Majesty came, Ifo-.' I stopped. I had to take the blame all by myself, did not dare land Ifor in any more trouble. 'When the King was here, Master Bleddyn said that if I could get out of the house without being caught, and could find a place where I could see without being seen, I might see the King. And I did! I climbed the big tree by the Knot Garden, and I saw the King!' *And he saw me, too!* I thought. 'Bleddyn Cook was being kind, Mrs Ann, because I was so disappointed that I shouldn't see the King. Don't be angry with Bleddyn Cook.'

Mrs Ann's eyebrows almost vanished into her white cap. 'You *what?* Master Bleddyn allowed – and after Master Mathias had forbidden you!'

'Oh, please let me finish, please, Mrs Ann. Please?'

Mrs Ann sniffed. 'I am shocked, Tirion Griffiths, I shall certainly have words with Master Bleddyn and –'

'Please, Mrs Ann, please listen to me! While I was up there, up the tree, that is, I saw a nest, and it made me think, and I was awake all the whole night wondering, and so as soon as I could get away, I went out again, and I climbed the tree again in all the thunder and lightning, and I was so scared, Mrs Ann, but all the same I climbed all the way up to the nest, and it was a magpie, and I chased it away, and a squirrel scared me so much I nearly fell out of the tree, and then the lightning flashed right over and then I did fall out, right on my bum, but –' I fumbled in my pocket, produced my cap, and unwrapped the treasures inside. 'Look, Mrs Ann! The magpie stole the Master's silver buttons. It wasn't Ifor! Ifor isn't a thief!'

Mrs Ann gazed at me as if I had grown another nose. She peered into the cap, and poked the buttons and the other things as if she could hardly believe her eyes. 'Well I never!' Her face softened. 'Tirion, I think I might have to forgive you. I shall go and see the Mistress at once. The Master will be pleased to have his buttons back, but not as pleased as I am that we do not have a thief in the House. Wait here and do not move a step.'

And so I waited, my heart pounding with relief. Ifor slouched in, his face as miserable as a wet fair-day, and glanced at me. 'What's the matter with you? Your face is white as a Monday sheet,[3] and you have two red spots on your cheeks.'

'You'll find out,' I said, mysteriously. 'But it's good, I promise.'

Mrs Ann came back after a while.

'Tirion, you are to go to the Withdrawing Room at once. The Mistress wants to see you. Go on with you, hurry now – no, come here.' She straightened my cap and tucked a strand of hair inside. 'Change your

---

[3] Monday was washing day, so all the sheets were white on Monday!

apron – here's a clean one. There's a smudge on your nose.' She spat on her kerchief and wiped the smudge. 'Go on. Hurry.'

When I reached the Withdrawing Room, the Master and the Mistress were there together. My heart began to pound like a drum, and my face turned red as a cherry. I wished the floor would open and I could disappear. I twisted my hands in my pinny and toed the carpet. I hardly dared look at them.

'My goodness,' the Mistress said, 'what is this tale I have heard? It seems you are to be thanked, Tirion Griffiths. Although,' she frowned, sternly, 'I should prefer that you did not climb any more trees. Especially –'

'– when His Majesty is walking below them,' the Master finished, frowning. 'I am pleased to have my silver buttons back. They were my father's before me, and I was sorry indeed to lose them. But you deserve a reward, Tirion Griffiths. What shall it be?'

At last I looked up. A reward! Now was my chance. My chance to get away from the hated spiders forever. My chance to tell the Master and Mistress that I was a person of learning, who could read and write and count, was not just a spider-brusher and greasy pot-scrubber. This was my chance to rise in the world. To be someone a bit important, at last. All I had to do was ask . . .

'If you please, Master, Sir,' I said, shyly. 'Please, may Ifor be allowed to work with your horses, Sir, and not be a spit-boy any more? He wants to be a groom like Jenkin Jones one day, when he has learned how, but because Master Mathias thought he was a thief, he is still a spit-boy, Sir. And he isn't a thief, Sir, is he, Sir? If you please, Sir. May Ifor be a groom? If you please, Sir?'

* I shall try to have nothing at all to do with her head-lice –
** – or with collecting wee from newborn babies or mouse skin eyebrows and things.
*** But I haven't forgiven him yet. I shall still take my Revenge when I can. *And it will be terrible when it comes . . .*

My Journal

Well, Mam, here is good News for you. I have not been at Llancaiach Fawr even a year, yet, and Already I have been promoted! The Mistress has made me one of her chamber-Maids, and I shall learn to dress her hair* and take care of her skin** and her fine Clothes. It is a very great honour and I shall earn more Money that I will send Home to you.

Also, my friend Ifor, who used to be the spit-boy, will not have to get hot and sweaty and sometimes burned turning the spit that cooks the meat any more, because now he will work with the horses.

Please tell your Husband my Stepfather that even though he made me be a Spider-brusher, I worked hard and have Got on.***

A Bit of Background

Llancaiach Fawr Manor is a little like a Time Machine. Thanks to the people who have restored it so beautifully, and the people who look after it from day to day, and those who 'become' the people who once lived in the house, we are able to imagine what life was like in the seventeenth century.

However, everything at Llancaiach happens in one year – 1645. Because of this, the English Civil War (it's always called 'English' even though it affected an awful lot of Welsh people as well) isn't really the main theme of the house. Llancaiach is a reconstruction of a way of life – and in this book I have tried to give you an idea of what life might have been like for a servant in a great house in 1645.

Because of this one-year time period, the Civil War doesn't play a great part in the book, although it is always there in the background. Civil Wars are terrible things, because they take place between two lots of arguing people in the same country. Even within families people have different opinions and loyalties, and sometimes the War meant that brother was fighting brother, or father fighting son. Even at Llancaiach there were different opinions among the servants, and Colonel Prichard himself changed sides towards the end of the War, beginning as a Royalist (or Cavalier) and ending as a Parliamentarian (or Roundhead). There is a very funny spoof history book, called *1066 and All That* which describes the Royalists as being 'Wrong but Wromantic', and the Parliamentarians as 'Right and Repulsive'. However, the main cause of the Civil War was King Charles I himself.

He was a very vain and arrogant (bossy) sort of person, and the War that he started in 1642 ended only with his execution. That wasn't a popular thing for Cromwell to do – an English King had never had his head chopped off before (well, not by an executioner, anyway – although several were murdered in various ways!). But his death probably saved the lives of lots of ordinary people, because it ended the War.

The problem was that King Charles I, like his father, King James I, believed in the Divine Right of Kings. He believed that only God could make a King, and since God had decided to make him King Charles I of England, any laws or demands or orders that Charles made should be treated as if they had come from God Himself. Since God, of course, is always right, so, therefore, must the King be!

This didn't make Charles very popular, especially with the Parliament of the time. Just like today, Parliament then was full of Members sent there to represent places all over Britain, and those Members of Parliament (MPs) were there to make sure that people were taxed fairly, and weren't treated badly, by the King and other powerful people.

Charles I used to offer to sell people Honours – that is, he would make them a Sir or a Lord or a Duke – if they paid him a lot of money. If they said, no thank you very much, he fined them the same amount of money they would have paid for the honour! In the end Parliament got fed up with him and began to say 'no' quite a lot, so King Charles had a tantrum and locked and bolted the doors of the House of Commons for eleven years – called 'The Eleven Years of Tyranny'.

From then on, Charles ruled all by himself, without any help from Parliament, using the Court of Star Chamber, in which, because he was ruling by Divine Right, he (of course) always won.

King Charles always needed money – he was very extravagant – and he kept finding different ways of getting it. One way was Ship Money, which helped pay for the Navy. At one time Ship Money only had to be paid by people who lived near the coast and were likely to be attacked (by the Dutch, or the French, or the other European people who didn't Get On with England then). But King Charles decided that everyone should have to pay it, wherever they lived, which wasn't at all popular.

He also upset the Scottish people, by telling them that they had to use a new prayer book, and in 1639 Scotland got so cross with him that they attacked England. This had one good result, because King Charles had to recall Parliament – because only Parliament could give him enough money to fight a war, and England needed defending.

However, in 1642 Charles got very fed up with five MPs in particular, who were being really Difficult and saying no to him a lot. So he took 300 soldiers and went to the Houses of Parliament to arrest them – but they had been warned and had already left to hide in the City of London. King Charles, when he arrived, is supposed to have said, 'I see the birds have flown'.

Six days after trying to arrest the MPs, Charles I left London to ride to Oxford to raise an army to fight Parliament for control of England.

And the Civil War began.

The Battle of Naseby

King Charles I visited Llancaiach Fawr Manor in 1645 because he was staying at Raglan Castle in Monmouthshire. He had been defeated at a battle on 14th June at a place called Naseby, in Northamptonshire, and had retreated to Raglan.

The Royalists were led by Prince Rupert of the Rhine,[1] and the Parliamentarians by Sir Thomas Fairfax.

Prince Rupert (when he finally arrived, perhaps with ice-cream on his moustache) started the battle in a really good position. He was on top of a high ridge looking down on the Parliamentarian army. It is very hard to fight a battle uphill, because the soldiers are climbing up towards people above them – who could quite easily ding them on top of the head and kill them, or at least make them completely lose interest in fighting any more.

Cromwell and Fairfax decided to move their army towards Naseby Ridge, about four miles away, and as soon as Rupert saw this, he got over-confident,

---

[1] See footnote, page 86

and decided to attack. He left his good position to swoop down on the Parliamentarians. At first the Roundhead cavalry were pushed back, and the infantry soon followed, but then Cromwell's horsemen wheeled round and attacked the Royalists from the side. There were many, many more Parliamentarians than there were Royalists, and Prince Rupert's silly mistake (perhaps he was Showing Off) caused him to lose the battle.

The Roundheads chased the Cavaliers for twelve miles from Naseby and killed every single one they caught. They captured the Royalist supplies – their food and their weapons, and also the King's private papers. These revealed that the King planned to bring in Catholic soldiers from Ireland (Charles was a Catholic, the Parliamentarians were mainly Protestant) and foreign mercenaries (soldiers who would fight for anyone if they were paid enough), to fight the War, which was sort of cheating.

Parliament instantly published the papers, and everyone in England was so cross about it that the Battle of Naseby was probably the beginning of the end for the Wrong but Wromantic Cavaliers.

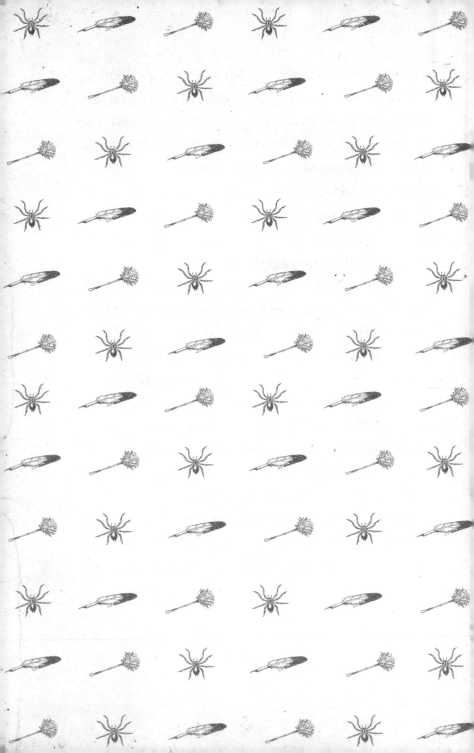